BATTLE HAREM

BOOK THREE

ISAAC HOOKE

BOOKS BY ISAAC HOOKE

Military Science Fiction

Battle Harem

Battle Harem 1

Battle Harem 2

Battle Harem 3

AI Reborn Trilogy

Refurbished

Reloaded

Rebooted

ATLAS Trilogy

(published by 47North)

ATLAS

ATLAS 2

ATLAS 3

Alien War Trilogy

Hoplite

Zeus

Titan

Argonauts

Bug Hunt

You Are Prey

Alien Empress

Quantum Predation

Robot Dust Bunnies

City of Phants

Rade's Fury

Mechs vs. Dinosaurs

A Captain's Crucible

Flagship

Test of Mettle

Cradle of War

Planet Killer

Worlds at War

Space Opera

A Cold Day in Mosul

Terminal Phase

Visit IsaacHooke.com for more information.

CONTENTS

1

J ason stepped back as Xin spun toward him. Her eyes flared brightly, warning him of the impending attack. He managed to amp up his Bullet Time and duck just as she released her lethal plasma beam. It struck the outside of his chest in a glancing blow, melting some of the armor there, but he avoided most of the blast as he hit the ground.

Beside Xin, Aria also turned her lightning weapon on him at the same time and struck his upper arm with a powerful bolt. It tore into the slug processing compartment of his left bicep, drilling a hole right through, emptying all of the pre-processed slugs in the process and disabling the weapon.

Sophie, Tara and Lori immediately interceded. Sophie activated her jumpjets and leaped on Aria; her micro machines, shaped like a hammer, slammed into Aria at the same time. Tara materialized in front of Xin and swung her sword, forcing Xin to deactivate her beam and dodge the blow. Lori released plasma bolts at Xin as well.

Jason used the distraction to scramble to his feet and get his bearings.

The mechs of the new girls, Cheyanne, Maeran, and Iris, stood in place meanwhile, as if unsure of what to do. They had been hanging out with Aria and Xin, along with all the other girls, each night in VR, so they probably considered the two of them friends by now. But they had also agreed to follow Jason, since he had set them free of Bokerov. He didn't blame them for not knowing whose side to take.

"We can't let you betray humanity!" Aria transmitted. "By joining the Tyrnari!"

"I only plan to join them for a little while!" Jason said. "We'll eventually turn on them." He told her that mostly to placate her, because in truth he still wasn't precisely certain what he wanted to do when it came to the invaders, other than avoid fighting them.

"And how long is a little while?" Aria said, blocking the next attack from Sophie with her ballistic shield. "After the alien army has marched across the world, with you at their side?"

"No!" Jason said. He ducked a lightning bolt attack that Aria unleashed from the side of her shield. "Of course not. I just want to buy us some time!" He gestured toward the massive army emerging through the rift in front of him. "We can't fight this."

"Can't we?" Aria said. Sophie scored a hit with her micro machines, digging into Aria's side. She swung her shield to the left, cutting off the successive flow of the machines, exposing her flank to Jason's energy weapon. But he couldn't bring himself to fire.

"I told you, you must lead them with an iron will," Bokerov commented over the comm band. "They only respond to dominance. See what happens when you show weakness?"

"Lori, please tell me you can shut them down remotely with those hacking skills of yours," Jason said.

"No," Lori said. "I unfortunately showed them all the vulnerabilities in their codebases. They've patched them. I could look for some zero day backdoors, but that could take quite a while."

Aria smashed her shield into Sophie, knocking her mech to the ground. Xin meanwhile had broken away from Lori and Tara, and she leaped toward Jason, superheating her hull in the process. She revolved in mid leap, spinning rapidly until she became that living drill she was so fond of forming.

Jason tried to leap aside in Bullet Time, but he was going to take at least a glancing hit, if not worse.

But then Maeran intervened. Or rather, her drones. She sent them forward in a triangular pattern in front of him, with a force field of energy between them.

Xin hit the shield that had formed in front of him, and her mech bounced away harmlessly.

Aria broke free of Sophie, and turned her lightning bolt weapon on Jason.

Before she could fire, energy whips shot out from Iris's locust mech, and wrapped around the weapon. She'd obviously dialed down the power output of those whips, because Jason had seen them cut through metal, and right now they simply held the weapon fast. Iris yanked on the whips and redirected the muzzle so that the lightning bolt passed just over Jason's head.

It looked like the new girls had chosen their side.

That pleased him immensely.

During all of this, the Tyrnari troops and vessels emerging from the rift ignored the fighting. Some of them passed within only a few hundred meters, as the forefront of the Tyrnari army moved in front of the vanguard of Jason's own. Apparently the aliens weren't too surprised that the Bokerovs would be fighting amongst themselves.

Aria tugged at her lightning weapon, trying to break free of Iris' whips. Lori came up behind Aria, and wrapped her arms around her chest, further subduing her.

Sophie and Tara meanwhile grabbed Xin, and kept her from pointing those plasma beams at Jason.

Meanwhile, the other Arias and Xins weren't interfering, and remained quiet. Jason's own clones seemed better at managing the women than himself. He'd have to ask them what their secret was.

Wait a moment, not so fast.

Aria 2 and Xin 2, as well as Aria 3 and Xin 3, were subdued at the moment by other members of their respective War Forgers. Only Jerry and Julian had kept their teams under control.

Well, good for them.

Aria suddenly stopped struggling. She gazed at the Tyrnari troops passing by behind her and cocked her head. "You know what, let's talk this out."

"Good choice," Jason said.

"I can't think with the buzzing of these energy whips…" Aria said.

"Iris, let her go," Jason said. "Lori, keep her restrained for—"

Iris' whips went slack, and before Jason could finish, Aria smashed Lori away from her. At the same time, Xin broke free of Sophie and Tara, and together the two of them ran toward the closest group of Tyrnari. Aria and Xin emitted friendly signatures just like everyone else, so of course the Tyrnari did nothing as they closed.

"Damn it!" Jason said. "Stop them!"

But it was already too late: Aria and Xin were already firing upon the alien troops.

Jason aimed his energy weapon at Aria, but once again couldn't bring himself to pull the trigger. Bokerov didn't have any such qualms, however, and began unleashing plasma bolts and missiles their way.

Evading, Aria and Xin dove into the heart of the alien troops, causing some of those bolts and missiles to strike the Tyrnari.

"Bokerov, tell the aliens we're having a minor malfunction with some of our units!" Jason said.

Aria and Xin had entered a group of Phaser mechs, who turned to face them.

Meanwhile, other troops began to mobilize. On his overhead map, Jason saw flashes appearing all throughout his ranks, indicating where members of Bokerov's army were taking fire.

It was too late.

Bokerov confirmed as much. "They've stopped answering my communications. Most likely, they're thrilled about this… I'm certain they were looking for an opportunity to renege on their agreement to give me their technology. And now, thanks to your undisciplined harem, you've given them one."

The Phaser mechs produced swords that launched lightning bolts. A circular red outline appeared over Jason, marking the target zone of one of those weapons, and he dove to the side as a huge lightning bolt tore through the air where he had stood.

Some of those Phasers were equipped with rocket launchers. Jason's missile alarm activated, and he fired his Battle Cloak countermeasure, detonating several of the munitions early. When they exploded, the missiles left behind floating, amorphous black blobs in the air. Those blobs moved outward, seeking out different members of Bokerov's army. Jason watched as a tank was enveloped, and the mass seemed to harden, freezing the tank in place. A lightning bolt struck it a moment later, and the entire black mass shattered into a thousand pieces.

Artillery units in another regiment behind the Phasers began to lob shells. These artillery were white in color, and egg-shaped, floating a meter off the ground. They had small rectangular sections protruding from the top, with small dark circles indicating the weapons those rectangles were armed with. Like the other alien units, there was one circle each for plasma, laser, and energy attacks, and a fourth for the particular brand of shells the aliens utilized.

When those shells hit the ground, there was no explosion, but rather everything within a sphere five meters in diameter utterly disintegrated. Holes in the shape of perfect half-spheres were left behind in the ground, replacing the units that had once stood there.

"It's time to fight, War Forgers!" Jason said. He released several missiles. "Fire at will! Bokerov, engage! I hope you're happy now, Aria!"

"I am," Aria said.

"I always intended to fight, but not like this," Jason said. "You forced my hand early."

"Finally, I did something right." Aria was firing at the Phasers, along with Xin. They coordinated their attacks: Xin would release a weak plasma beam, causing a Phaser to wink out. And Aria would time her lightning bolt release to coincide with the Phaser's return to this reality.

"We could have engaged in guerrilla warfare, wearing them down over the coming weeks, but no, you had to go and attack them outright!" Jason said. "I tried to ensure we had a chance. But now look at us. Because of your reckless actions, you've endangered not just our army, but our entire world. We're on the losing side of a pitched battle. Badly outnumbered. With nowhere to run."

Aria didn't answer.

Well, there was no point in whining about it any further. What was done, was done.

It was time to fight.

Overhead, Bokerov's bombers made several flybys, and unleashed carpet bombs at enemy units.

Those bombs that targeted the Phasers were well-timed: the first bomb would hit, and there would be a one point two-five second delay before the second bomb impacted, coinciding with the reappearance of the Phasers.

Some of the alien flyers accelerated to engage the bombers. Equipped with plasma, energy, and laser weapons, these were the elliptical vessels that Jason and his team had encountered previously. The craft didn't seem to be affected by the limitations of gravity.

Bokerov dispatched some fighter jets to deal with them in turn.

Several towering airships turned toward the army. They looked like big, rectangular things, with slightly curved fronts. Like the flyers, they seemed unaffected by the laws of physics, at least when it came to maneuvering.

"Bokerov, move your Cataphracts into place!" Jason said.

The Axeman and Horse moved forward. The Axeman swung at one of those big ships, and cut it in half. The Horse, meanwhile, fired its energy beam into another ship, carving a huge hole.

But other nearby ships returned fire. The Axeman's right arm was hit with an energy blast, and the entire limb disintegrated. The Horse took several concentrated blows, riddling its body with craters. The big mech collapsed.

Bokerov's artillery were unleashing shells against the artillery units beyond the Phasers, while his tanks were firing lasers and plasma bolts at the big ships, which seemed the biggest threat at the moment.

"Aria, Xin, can I count on you to combine?" Jason asked.

No answer.

He couldn't just issue the combine command, and expect it to work. All of the mechs had to submit to the combination process, because it involved linking minds. Which was why he couldn't just combine earlier to get Aria and Xin under control.

"Aria—" Jason pressed.

"We'll combine," Aria said.

"All right, War Forgers, and clones," Jason said. "Combine!"

Jason switched to VR where the five girls were already waiting. They held hands in a circle, with Lori and Tara leaving a spot between them for him.

Jason went to them, held their palms, and accepted the energy pulses that they fed into his body. When those pulses reached his mind, his perception changed so that he was viewing the interlocking of all their neural networks and sharing all their memories, and their deepest, darkest secrets. He never knew them as well as he did when he was here. Unfortunately, most of that knowledge was lost when they separated, with only vague echoes remaining.

His vision returned to the real world, and the six mechs ran toward each other. Aria became the chest. Jason the head. Tara his right arm. Sophie his left arm. Lori his left leg. Xin his right leg. Weapons and body parts repositioned upon tracks. Aria's ballistic shield,

Tara's sword, and Lori's tail all enlarged, with help from Sophie's micro machines.

And then it was done. Jason had become a Cataphract. Beside him stood the other four Cataphracts of the clones, and Bokerov's non-combining Cataphracts.

The Rex Wolves howled on the ground beside him. Though they had grown in recent weeks, now they were back to the size of dogs, given his current height.

Jason dashed forward, leading the charge. He trampled the smaller troops underfoot; and waded through the larger Phasers. He easily deflected their attacks with his huge ballistic shield, and swung back with his sword. If the Phasers winked out, he'd continue onward, leaving them for the other Cataphracts and Rex Wolves behind him to finish off.

He approached one of the big hovering ships. While on the run, he fired the plasma beam from his right hip, the energy weapon on his right shoulder, plasma bolts from his tail, and lightning bolts from his left arm.

The rectangular ship shuddered under the blows, with portions of it falling away; Jason was close enough now to finish the job with his sword, so he swung the big blade, slicing right through the transport ship. The twin pieces dropped to the ground, revealing different decks inside like the insides of a doll house. Yellow mist vented outward as its atmosphere leaked.

The nearby rectangular ships were rotating his way, and he swiveled his ballistic shield in front of him as they returned fire.

The other Cataphracts, both the War Forgers and

Bokerov versions, engaged different enemies, including those rectangular ships, though some of the Cataphracts were bogged down by the smaller troops that surrounded them. Bokerov did his best to use his own small troops to defend against the latter.

A row of artillery units was firing shells and plasma bolts at point blank range against Bokerov's Dinosaur. That unit became riddle with holes as those shells detonated and disintegrated portions of the hull. The Cataphract wouldn't be able to hold up much longer under the impacts.

The Rex Wolves rushed in suddenly, plowing through those alien artillery as if they weighed nothing. Bruiser bit into one, crunching it in half. Lackey crushed another with his weight. Shaggy bashed one aside with his thick head, sending it flying into another armored unit. Runt meanwhile leaped on top of a tank and began chomping into its rectangular turret, breaking it away along with part of the hull below.

A squad, this one made of similar white, egg-shaped vessels, but these ones possessing elaborate treads rather than merely floating, turned their attention to the Rex Wolves.

No.

J ason weaved between the airships and slammed his shield down in front of the dogs just as those treaded vehicles opened fire. His shield turned red on the inside in several places as it took the blows.

The act left him open to attack from the side, and one of the airships lit into him. His right arm—Tara— was bombarded with energy blasts. He shifted, exposing his back—Aria—to the impacts.

Jerry intervened in his Cataphract, bringing his own shield to bear, and blocking the impacts.

"Thanks," Jason said. "I owe you one."

"Nope," Jerry said. "Paying you back for saving my girls last time."

Jason was still receiving fire from the treaded units, forcing him to remain in place to protect the Rex Wolves, who were occupied with the artillery.

The mechs of Cheyanne, Maeran, and Iris swept past him, heading toward the units firing at him.

Cheyanne used her wings to arc over Jason's shield, and landed among the attackers. The East Indian flung out her swords and swirled as she moved, cutting through the enemy like a spinning top. Her caramel-skinned avatar momentarily appeared in his HUD, biting her lower lip, the gold chain hanging from her nose to her ear swaying as she did so.

Maeran spat that gooey substance from her mech, gluing one of the alien tanks in place. The goo enveloped the turret and prevented the vehicle from firing. She spun to the right, sending her drones to intercept the attack from another tank, which had launched plasma bolts at her. The drones formed a triangular shield that deflected the blow, then moved forward. She must have amped up the intensity of the energy emitted by those drones, because when they passed the tank, the triangular beams formed by the three machines sliced the top portion of the hull right off.

Iris unleashed the energy whips she held in her four arms and cut through the rectangular turrets of different alien tanks. She crab-walked with her six legs, doing her best to avoid being struck by return fire.

The Rex Wolves finished with the artillery squad, and then raced past to join the three mechs.

Another airship came in, and it seemed ready to fire at the girls and the dogs.

Jason teleported in front of them—the range was just enough to reach the airship. He stabbed upward with the sword, cutting through the vessel and sending it plowing into the ground behind him. It formed a deep runnel as it crashed.

He cut his way forward in that manner, taking down airships as fast as he could, but there were always three more for every one he shot down. Sometimes, when he cut open a vessel, it proved to be a transport craft, and more troops flooded out before or after it crashed. The latest airship he felled, for example, released a hundred Phasers. They reached to his waist, and Jason found himself wading through the units, firing every weapon he was capable of, trying to get away from the horde so he could fight from a more defensible position. The alien mechs phased out on his attacks, so he started sweeping his sword first, and then followed up with shots from his lightning, energy, and plasma weapons.

When he finally broke free, he found himself surrounded by airships, and swung his sword frantically to take them down; he was able to get rid of three of them in short order, and raised his shield to protect himself against the other. Holes riddled the edges of the shield. It could take only a few more hits.

His power levels were also on the low side. He couldn't teleport anymore, nor turn invisible. He had just enough to create a body enveloping energy shield, but if he did that, he'd be close to zero.

"How's the power situation?" Jason asked.

He glanced at the War Forger team stats on his HUD, and had his answer. Almost everyone else was in the same power situation.

"Bombers!" John said.

Jason heard the high pitched keening of bombs. His HUD lit up with red circles that indicated the impact sites, however since the effects of the missiles were unknown, there was no darker circle specifying the blast radius.

"Put some distance between yourselves and those bombs!" Jason dashed away as bombs hit the area; these were more powerful than those launched by the artillery, and vaporized areas two hundred meters in diameter, creating deep craters in the ground.

"Z, update the blast radius settings on those bombs for next time!" Jason said.

"You got it," Z said in her sensual voice. Jason didn't bother to glance at the avatar that appeared. It'd be too distracting at the moment.

More bombs dropped. Most of Bokerov's army wasn't able to move out of the way in time, and they took a beating.

"I'm losing a lot of troops," Bokerov said. "Can't keep this up."

The Dinosaur and Torch had gone down, and Bokerov's other Cataphracts had sustained heavy damage. As for his smaller troops…

Jason glanced at the overhead map. The number of troops had dropped by half. Whereas the enemy was still thousands strong. And growing as more continued to flow through the rift.

A group of two legged alien mechs swarmed Cheyanne. They had swords, like some of the Phasers, and were laying into her from all sides. She attempted to take flight, but a Phaser had managed to grab onto her legs. She promptly activated her shockwave weapon, sending the attackers flying backward in every direction. Then she took flight, skimming low over the attackers.

"That was my last charge," Cheyanne said.

A plasma bolt struck her in the wing, and she promptly crashed into the ground. She stood up, and raised her sword to defend against a Phaser that came at her. Another Phaser fired a lightning bolt from its swords, and hit her in the side.

Jason finished taking down another airship, and rushed to her, but Maeran and Iris were already there, along with two of the Rex Wolves.

Jason spun as another airship came at him, firing everything it had, and deflected the blows with his shield. Jerry rammed his sword into that vessel, and it crashed, spilling out artillery.

Runt and Shaggy leaped into the fray, attacking the egg-shaped objects, chewing and bashing.

"We have to retreat!" Jones said. "You wanted to stage guerrilla warfare? That sounds like a good idea right about now."

"Retreat to where?" Tara said. "At least here, we have their airships and other troops partially shielding us. We run away, we'll be completely exposed to the full brunt of their weapons! They'll use their bombers to herd us into a kill zone, and bam! Bye-bye War Forgers. It's what I would do."

"Tell me again why Aria and Xin thought it was a good idea to draw us into this fight?" Sophie said.

A missile exploded nearby, close to John, and the black blob struck his arm, enveloping his sword, and part of his Tara.

"Damn it," John said.

He sought out the source, but Julian had already found it, and took down the airship. Five more were incoming behind it.

The lower part of John's arm abruptly broke away from the increased weight caused by the blob, and when it hit the ground, it shattered.

"Tara 2, you all right?" Jason asked, glancing at his HUD. Her Damage Report screen wasn't pretty.

"Lost my legs," Tara 2 said. "But I'll live."

As Jason ducked another plasma bolt, he realized Jones was right. The team had to retreat. There were simply too many attackers. It was obvious the War Forger army wasn't going to win this.

But where could they retreat to? Like Tara had said, they'd be completely exposed.

He surveyed the plains nearby. The fighting had swept the Cataphracts and most of Bokerov's army toward the southern side of the rift. Maybe they could circumnavigate it, and use the rip in spacetime as a shield of sorts to protect them from the sight lines of the rest of the alien army. But what happened when that rift winked out? Jason's army would be exposed all over again. Plus, it wouldn't take much effort for the aliens to reposition their troops to obtain a better firing angle.

But maybe there was another way.

Jason glanced at the rift. The atmosphere seeping from the alien homeworld formed a yellow mist that drifted well in front of the spacetime tear. Beyond, the alien units were no longer blackening the plains and air:

nearly all of them had entered from their staging area into this world, darkening the land and sky here instead.

Best of all, at the moment, there were only a few aliens lying between Jason's army, and the spacetime tear.

"We have to go through the rift!" Jason said. "It's our best chance of survival."

"You do know if we go through that rift, there's no coming back?" Sophie said.

"I'm aware of that," Jason said, deflecting another blow from a nearby airship. "But I can't see we have any other choice. There are too many of them here. Look through the rift... there are hardly any forces on the other side: they've all entered into our world. At least there, we have a chance. Once we pass through, we'll turn to the south, putting ourselves beyond the edge of the rift, and their line of fire, at least when viewed from this world."

"What's to stop them from simply following us through and finishing the job?" Tara said.

"I'm also guessing the Tyrnari can't hold the rift open for much longer," Jason said. "Inter-dimensional wormholes probably need a shit ton of energy to keep open, and I'm hoping they won't have *time* to follow! Sure, they'll send a few troops, probably. Maybe an airship or bomber, but I doubt any more than a handful of units will pursue. In fact, they'll probably be glad to be rid of us."

"I think you're right that they won't follow," Aria said. "But only because they'll assume whatever forces they have on the staging planet will simply take care of us. And those forces probably will."

"I agree," Xin said. "I don't think fleeing to an alien world is the solution."

"You always side with Aria," Jason said. "I've come to expect that by now. What is it with you two?"

He wasn't expecting an answer, and he didn't get one, because the team was distracted by more red circles that appeared over the ground: alien bombers had dropped their latest salvo. This time Z included the complete blast radius—it wasn't going to be pretty.

"Well, I'm going through the rift," Jason said. "I'm issuing a de-combine order. The rest of you can decide whether you want to stay here and retreat another way, or go with me. Bokerov, you don't get that choice. Your army is coming with me."

"Of course the Russian slave doesn't get the choice," Bokerov said.

"Next time don't make me force you to your knees," Jason said.

"Oh, you'll be the one on your knees the next time we spar," Bokerov said.

The micro machines separated from the hull of the Cataphract, and Jason's energy weapon slid along the track, back into place on his arm, as did his railgun. His bicep area was still damaged, so the railgun was useless.

He broke away as the de-combine continued, and he leaped to the ground, landing with a heavy thud. He tramped forward, firing his energy weapon at the few egg-shaped tanks that blocked his path. He also unleashed the last of his missiles.

Unsurprisingly, Tara joined him, as did Lori and Sophie. But he did admit to feeling a little shocked when Aria and Xin came to his side.

"If you all wanted to come, I could have stayed combined!" Jason said. Then again, they had a smaller profile now, which left them less open to attack, considering that the Phasers and other units behind them were about the same height.

The other War Forgers de-combined to reduce their profile as well, and all of them came, to the last man and woman. Bokerov's tanks and artillery followed behind the War Forgers, with the Cataphracts lumbering in the rear. Bokerov's remaining bombers and fighter jets tore through the yellow mist of the rift and swerved to the south, and out of the line of fire of the enemy units on this side.

The Rex Wolves dashed alongside Jason and Tara. They bit into or knocked aside any of the aliens mechs or tanks that blocked their path—none were Phasers. As the teams got closer to the rift, the yellow mist that had extended across the plains encircled their legs.

"What about the dogs?" Tara said. "We can't take them through! They won't survive the atmosphere on the other side!"

"Actually, they will," Aria said. "I've already sampled the atmosphere pouring from the rift, now that we're near. It matches the chemicals the bioweapons emitted in the early days of the last invasion. While there's some stuff in it that's harmful to Terran life, most of the mutants we've ever encountered have two pairs of lungs—the first so that they could exist in our pre-terraformed environment, the second intended to activate post-terraforming. I've come across my share of Rex Wolf corpses during my wanderings, and they're no different. I believe their second set of lungs will take over."

"What if you're wrong?" Tara said.

"Then they die," Aria said.

Jason was the first to reach the rift. He leaped through, fearful about tripping on the lower edge of the rift and getting a foot cut off. But he needn't have feared, as the bottom portion seemed to be embedded in the ground.

The others passed through behind him, along with Bokerov's surviving troops.

The alien troops and craft on this side unleashed salvos from their turrets, and Jason returned fire.

The different Arias directed their shields toward the enemy units, providing protection against the incoming fire.

The dogs beside Jason hadn't faltered in their gaits. Not one bit. They simply passed through the alien environment and continued running. Jason supposed it helped that there was sunlight on this side, at the top of that yellow sky. Though only a pinprick of light, it seemed just as intense as that of Earth's sun, at least based on his external temperature sensors.

The aliens continued assailing Jason and the others. Bokerov's bombers made a pass, eliminating a good swath of the attackers.

"This way!" Jason fled to the south, where a forest of psychedelic pine trees lined the horizon. The yellow mist of the atmosphere limited visibility somewhat, however, and he couldn't see as far as he would have liked into those trees.

Glancing at his rear view feed, he realized that not a one of the alien troops were bothering to pursue. They still continued to fire occasionally, but the attacks were halfhearted at best.

"It's like I said," Jason told the others. "The rift is closing soon. The Tyrnari want to get as many of their troops through as possible, and they're not worried about what mischief we might cause here."

"That's because the troops on this side have probably already radioed for reinforcements," Tara said.

"All the more reason to keep moving!" Jason said.

The Rex Wolves continued to do well beside him. He had to conclude that their lungs were indeed capable of filtering the air.

As Jason got closer to the trees, he realized just how massive they were. They towered at least twice as tall as their large mechs, and would easily give the team cover against attacks.

When Jason reached the southern edge of those huge pine trees, the alien attacks ceased. He glanced in his rear view feed and realized why: the last of the aliens had gone through the rift. As he watched, the rift vanished entirely.

"And so it's done," Cheyanne commented. "We've stranded ourselves on another world, giving up on humanity."

"Just as humanity gave up on us," Iris spat.

Jason paused for a moment to survey the forest.

"Well, we might as well go inside. At the very least, these trees will shield us from whatever reinforcements arrive. Who knows, maybe we'll even evade the alien search parties."

With that, Jason entered the forest.

3

J ason moved between the trunks of the great pines. There was enough room between them for the mechs to easily walk, sometimes two abreast. There was no real canopy, and sunlight readily reached their mechs, allowing them to power their batteries. The recharge rate only confirmed his previous theory regarding the sun's strength: it was on par with Earth's, even though it seemed way smaller in the sky.

Jason activated his repair swarm so that he could begin repairs while he walked. Other units in the army did the same, including Bokerov's. The repair drones were equipped with obstacle avoidance, and target tracking, so they could fix things on the move. The repairs were a bit slower while on the move, though, because of all the tracking overhead required.

John was carrying his Tara clone over his shoulders, since she had no legs for walking. The clones in other War Forger parties were similarly helping each other, with an Aria using the shoulders of a Sophie as a crutch, and so forth, while the repair drones did their work.

The undergrowth trampled easily underfoot, and the main teams cleared a path for the tanks behind them. Said foliage appeared to be mostly sticks of wood, with multi-colored spider webs threading between them.

"Must be some sort of lichen," Aria commented, scooping up a sample with one big finger.

The pines were coated in similar webbing, and when Jason looked closely, he realized those weren't pine needles at all, but silk-like purplish extensions that covered the many branches.

"That almost looks like hair, or fur," Iris said, herself examining one of the pines.

"Is that what you say when you take off your pants?" Lori asked. "Just kidding!"

"No one's laughing," Iris said. As usual, the Middle Eastern woman's avatar wore a pink shawl over her head, and a liberal dose of digital makeup.

"I know," Lori said. "I say the most inappropriate things, at the most inappropriate times. Sorry!"

"No, it is a good change," Maeran said. The Ethiopian's avatar was smiling, which made her face seem to radiate, framed as it was by that coiffure of tumbling curls, and the segmented chain that outlined her hairline. "These two can be so serious at times."

"That's because we were slaves," Iris said. She crab-walked around a tree with her six-legged Locust mech. "Which is no laughing matter."

"No, I suppose not," Maeran said. She pulled in her

orbiting drones to pass between two trunks that were spaced relatively close together. "But we are free now."

"Are we?" Cheyanne said. The red dot in the center of her forehead looked particular bright on her avatar at the moment, almost like a third eye. "And look at where this freedom brought us, We've blindly followed this man across the galaxy, believing that he would do what was best for us, and now we're trapped on some faraway world, with no hope of ever returning home."

"I kind of like that idea," Lori said. "Because to be honest, to me, I'm home wherever he is."

"As am I," Tara said.

"You two would say that," Sophie said.

Jason still hadn't slept with her since that one time she'd sneaked into his bed, pretending to be Tara. He probably should work things out between her and the other girls soon, since tensions between the three of them were running relatively high at the moment.

"He did save us," Iris said. "We owe him for that."

Cheyanne's avatar nodded, causing her nose chain to sway. "Yes. He saved us from oppression, but that doesn't mean we have to follow him across the galaxy."

"You came willingly," Jason reminded her. "I gave you all the choice to stay."

"It wasn't much of a choice!" Cheyanne sniffed. "We could have stayed, as you say, and allowed ourselves to be shot down by an alien army. Or go with you, and become trapped on an alien world."

"Then you should have left before coming with me to the rift," Jason said.

Cheyanne had nothing to say to that. She knew he was right.

But then she spoke a moment later. "Yes, he saves us from oppression, but then insults us, by keeping the oppressor among us!"

"Ah, I know what you are now," Jason said. "You're the complainer of the group. The nag."

"How dare——"

"And as for Bokerov," Jason interrupted. "I need him."

"I'm ready to oppress them again whenever you require me to," Bokerov said.

"That won't be necessary," Jason said. "In fact, I want you to never bring that up again. It's like you were joking. And what you did to them was anything but funny, is that clear?"

Bokerov didn't answer.

"Is that clear..." Jason repeated.

"*Da,*" Bokerov said. "Is clear." He lowered his voice. "Bitch."

"What did you say?" Jason asked.

"Oh, nothing," Bokerov said. "Just Russian word for sir."

"I somehow doubt 'bitch' is Russian for sir," Jason said. "In fact, I just looked it up. And it's not even close."

"Is special dialect of Russian," Bokerov insisted.

"And why are you suddenly pretending your English is broken?" Jason said. "When up until this point you've spoken English flawlessly?"

"I'm not pretending," Bokerov said. "Sometimes I

fall into my old dialect. I wasn't always an AI core, you know."

"None of us were," Jason agreed.

The group continued wandering. Jason still had his Explorer intact, and he launched it from a storage compartment in his leg. The Rex Wolves had grown used to the drone by now, and didn't bother to bark at it or even chase it.

Jason also had access to the feeds from the fighters and bombers Bokerov had in the region.

"I just remembered, the fuel on those craft isn't self-regenerating," Jason said.

"No, it's not," Bokerov said. "We should probably land them, considering we most likely won't find a compatible fuel source on this planet."

"You could have reminded me sooner," Jason said.

"Not my job," Bokerov said.

Jason shook his head. "I wonder if I should get Lori to tighten up your Containment Code a bit. Make you more pliant."

"Feel free," Bokerov said. "It will only make me work to break free of you all the harder."

"You really should enable your avatar sometime," Jason said. "Your *real* avatar, I mean. Because sometimes I can't tell if you're joking."

"That's the way I like it," Bokerov said.

Jason had commanded Bokerov to enable his avatar at one point previously, and Bokerov had displayed an ancient puzzle known as a Rubik's cube in place of a human face. Whenever Bokerov talked, a portion of the cube would solve itself. Annoying as hell.

"All right, land the aircraft," Jason said. "Choose a site close to the forest, if possible." He recalled how the terrain had looked on the way to the forest, and it seemed relatively flat. "Mark the landing site as a waypoint on our overhead maps."

"As you wish," Bokerov said.

Jason glanced at his overhead map. The terrain had filled in around him, courtesy of Bokerov's aircraft. It would continue to do so because of the Explorer he'd launched, but at a slower rate. Onboard mapping software would convert the video images into the 3D data necessary for their HUDs. The Explorer recharged via sunlight, so in theory it could scout ahead for as long as the army was on the march.

The map software used a coordinate system that designated their point of arrival on this planet as latitude zero and longitude zero.

"Z, how come our coordinates reset to zero after we passed through the rift?" Jason asked. "Shouldn't the coordinates have continued on from where we lost contact with the GPS satellites? As would happen on Earth?" Even without satellites, those coordinates would continue to update based on the positional data recorded by their own accelerometers and gyroscopes, rather than any satellites in orbit.

"Ordinarily the coordinates would continue from where they left off, yes," Z said. "But as we are no longer on Earth, I took the liberty to reset our coordinates to zero the instant we arrived. I've talked with the other Accomps and they've agreed this is the best course of action. Bokerov has agreed to the same reset."

"Oh," Jason said. "Thanks for asking for my permission first."

"My apologies," Z said. Her avatar appeared contrite. "It seemed like an appropriate change. Would you like me to reset our coordinates to match those we had before leaving Earth?"

"No, resetting the coordinates makes some sense," Jason said. "Considering that we don't know how big this planet is. It could be the size of a small moon. Or a super earth."

"Actually, gravity is very close to one G," Z said. "Which implies a size at least similar to Earth. That said, this could still be a moon, albeit a very large one."

"True enough," Jason said.

He activated his rear-view video feed. Following behind his War Forgers was Bokerov's host of surviving tanks and artillery, with the Cataphracts bringing up the rear: the Axeman, the Lizardman, the Octopus, the Sphinx, the Cobra, the Rifleman, the Caterpillar. Bokerov had ordered the units to crouch, so that they didn't protrude as much from the trees, but the resounding thuds made by their heavy footsteps could still be felt from Jason's position. The noise made by his own War Forgers wasn't any quieter.

The Rex Wolves kept pace on either side of his War Forgers, with Bruiser and Lackey staying close to Tara as usual, Runt mirrored Lori, and Shaggy stuck to Jason. The War Forger clones walked on either side in uncombined form. The different Tara clones sometimes glanced his way longingly, and at first it was because he thought they missed him, but then he realized it was the Rex Wolves they missed.

In moments, a waypoint appeared on the map. It was along the outskirts of the forest, as mapped by Bokerov's aircraft. When the last of the jets and bombers landed, their signals winked out, because of interference from the forest: there was no network of repeaters here, like Bokerov had set up on Earth.

"Did they land okay?" Jason asked the Russian.

"Yes," Bokerov said. "They've landed just fine. The terrain was a little bumpy, but nothing my high-quality landing gears couldn't handle."

"Of course," Jason said. "Everything you make is high quality."

"Very good," Bokerov said. "You're finally catching on."

Ahead, humongous flowers were set among the pines: the best analog was daisies, but with orange petals and black cores.

"These are some ugly flowers," Sophie commented.

"Not at all!" Lori said. "They look like sunflowers!"

"Hardly," Sophie said. "Look at the gashes in their cores. They look more like they could eat you than anything else."

Jason kept his particular group of War Forgers well clear of them, as did most of the others, save for Jerry, whose clones traveled the closest to them. The Aria of his group seemed curious about the large flowering plants, and she walked directly up to one of them.

The core opened up as she neared, and the stem

swayed, bringing the core and its petals down toward her head. The core opened up, revealing a wide maw.

Aria 5 leaped away, almost smashing into Jerry. The head swerved, following her movements, forcing both Aria 5 and Jerry to vault away from the flower. The core attempted to chomp down on their mechs but missed. The two mechs, and the other clones in Jerry's group, moved out of its reach.

"Cripes!" Jerry said. "Damn thing nearly ate my head off!"

"Stay away from the big flowers, people," Jason said.

The Rex Wolves barked wildly at the flower, but wisely kept their distance.

"Easy, Bruiser," Tara said, pulling on the fur beneath the dog's T-Rex-like head.

"These are suitable flowers to give to your girls," Bokerov said. "Nice and nasty. Just like them."

"Anyone mind if we mute Bokerov off the comm line for the time being?" Sophie 5 said.

"Feel free," Jason said. He kept his line open to the Russian, however, in case he needed to issue any orders.

Tara moved on, finally yanking Bruiser and Lackey away.

Jason kept walking, and Shaggy eventually lost interest in the deadly flower and joined him once more. Runt did the same with Lori.

"That was a fun fight we had back there, by the way, before we entered the rift," Bokerov said. "So I do thank you for the entertainment. But I'm still going to back-stab you whenever I get the chance."

"You do that," Jason told him.

"You ruined my chances of acquiring any alien technology," Bokerov said. "That's not something I can forgive. You Shit Forgers—"

"All right, guess I've had enough," Jason said. He decided to mute Bokerov after all. He'd simply reopen it if he needed to relay any orders.

Jason gazed through the colorful webbed trees ahead. The terrain seemed the same as far as the eye could see.

"All right, Z," he addressed his Accomp. "I think I'm going to head over to my VR. Care to man the ship for a while?"

"I'd be happy to," Z said.

"I want you to keep marching," Jason said. "I want to put as much distance between the rift site and ourselves as possible."

"If reinforcements arrive, they'll simply track our path through the forest, you realize this, right?" Z said. "An army traveling through a forest doesn't leave an invisible trail..."

"That's very true," Jason said.

"And if this staging area is a planet of any value to the Tyrnari, they likely have satellites in orbit that are tracking us now as we speak," Z said.

"Also true," Jason said. "But even so, it makes me feel better. Stay in the forest if you can, and steer clear of those flowers. Rouse me if you encounter anything new, or if the forest ends."

"Will do," Z said.

Jason switched to the public channel. "I'm logging into VR for a while, and setting my mech to Accomp control. Feel free to send me a message if you need anything. John, you're in command of the army."

"You got it," John said.

Drones still buzzed around him, continuing the repairs to his mech, as he logged out of reality.

4

J ason sat on the picnic table in front of the mountain lake. He gazed at the reflection of the sun as it was broken into a thousand shards by the shimmering water. Ordinarily, the water should have been still, but he swapped its texture for that of a stream today, and as he watched it flow, and listened to it gurgle, he felt immensely relaxed. He needed that, after the earlier events. He didn't know what he was going to do. It might not have been the best idea to travel through the rift and to an alien staging area, but it had seemed like the best choice at the time.

Now, he wasn't so sure. It might have been better to allow his army to be mowed down by the aliens, and hope that one of them survived long enough to dispatch the repair drones.

"Well, I made my choice," Jason said softly. "And I'll deal with the consequences. I just hope the girls can forgive me."

"There's nothing to forgive," Xin said from beside the picnic table. She, too, was gazing out at the lake / stream.

"How long have you been standing there?" Jason asked.

"Not long," the Japanese woman admitted.

"About the same length of time as me," another voice said from the other side of the picnic table. Aria. She was looking like her usual vampire self: pale skin, red lips, sapphire blue eyes. Minus the fangs she some-times wore.

Jason shook his head. "You two."

"Us," Aria said. "We owe you an apology. Not just you, but the entire team. We'll get to them. But we thought we'd do you, first."

"*Do* me?" Jason said. "Why do I like the sound of that?"

Aria smiled patiently, and glanced at Xin. Her expression read: *boys*.

"You shouldn't have attacked the aliens," Jason said.

"I'm sorry," Aria said. "I did the wrong thing. I realize that now. This is why it's a bad idea to put a civilian into a military war machine."

"Yes," Jason said. "Except in your case, I'm sure the military assumed that your Containment Code would never be lifted, and they'd have you on a tight leash."

"It's not easy controlling a bunch of girls who have minds of their own, is it?" Aria said.

"It's not so much that I want to control you," Jason said. "It's that I want you to do the right thing. And attacking the aliens back there definitely wasn't the right thing. You forced my hand. Made me do something I wasn't yet ready to commit to. You could have just attacked me, and got your frustrations out. The rest of the team would have subdued you, and none of this would have ever happened."

"You're right," Aria said. "But I already admitted I did the wrong thing. I let my emotions get the better of me: I probably should have dialed them down. It seemed, at the time, the only way to save humanity. Because you know, I actually thought we could win."

"So did I," Xin said. "I was overconfident in our abilities. And I admit, I wasn't thinking rationally when I followed Aria into the attack against the aliens. I, too, had my emotions online. I was only just beginning to grow comfortable with them, and decided to leave them enabled. It was a mistake. I can see that now. I've permanently turned my emotions off."

"No," Jason said. "Don't do that. Don't ever do that. Your emotions are the only thing making you human."

"If being human means attacking you," Xin said. "Then I don't want to be anything close to human. Looking back, I'm so ashamed of what I did. So ashamed. I care about you, so much, and yet I attacked you. It's... not right."

"Turn on your emotions," Jason said.

She stared at him, but then nodded. "It's done."

"How do you feel?" Jason asked.

"Like crying," Xin said. She had tears in her eyes.

"Remember that feeling the next time you want to betray me," Jason said. "Maybe you'll think twice before doing it."

"Can things ever be the same between us?" Xin asked.

Jason stared into her eyes, feeling a sudden longing for her touch. All of this was fake, of course, but it seemed so real to his mind.

Xin glanced at Aria, and seemed suddenly embarrassed. "I mean, can you ever trust me again? Me and Aria."

"Not right away," Jason said. "You'll have to earn that trust back."

"But we fought at your side," Aria said. "Combined with you."

"Yes, because you had to," Jason said. "After stirring up the proverbial wasps nest."

"No, we didn't have to," Aria said slowly. "We could have abandoned you at any time. We could have refused to combine, if we wanted to do you harm."

"You seemed like you were trying to do me harm before you attacked the aliens…" Jason told her softly.

"No," Aria said. "We would have never hurt you. At least not permanently."

"She's right," Xin said. "That was never our intention. We meant to dissuade you from joining the Tyrnari, nothing more."

"Oh," Jason said. "Nothing more. That's why when you couldn't make any headway against me, you went ahead and attacked the aliens."

"As I told you, we made a mistake," Aria said. "How many times do you want me to admit it? Would it help if I dropped to my knees and begged?"

Jason gave her a mischievous look. "It might."

She shook her head and looked away.

Jason shrugged. "I could expel you both from my army if I wanted to. There are other Arias and Xins I could replace you with. More obedient versions that didn't attack me, or the clones of myself."

"Yes there are," Aria said. "And replacing us would certainly be your prerogative, if that was what you chose."

He smiled sadly. "Except I could never do that."

"Why?" Aria said.

"What do you think?" Jason said. He gazed into Aria's sapphire eyes. So deep. So mysterious. He had known all of her secrets only a short while ago, while combined, but those secrets were gone now, lost when they separated, mere echoes.

"I have no idea," Aria said, though her voice rasped slightly, as if to hint at the fact that yes, she did know.

Jason stood up from the bench to sit down on the picnic table itself; he swiveled his legs around to the other side so that he was facing the lake. He patted the empty wood beside him, beckoning for Aria to sit down. He also did the same for Xin on the other side.

Aria sat down beside him, pressing her thigh against his. Xin sat on his other side, but she kept more of a demure distance. Their knees were bent at ninety degree angles over the edge of the table, and rested on the bench.

When the girls were both seated, Jason gazed out upon the lake. He replaced the texture with the standard lake variant so that the waters were still and the sun's reflection was no longer broken into a thousand fragments.

"It's so very blue," Jason said.

"Yes," Aria said.

"Like your eyes." Jason turned his head toward Aria. "No, scratch that. Nothing could ever match the beauty of these eyes." Aria was gazing at him, but her expression suddenly melted, becoming almost like a puppy dog's.

She glanced at his lips, and he took that as the invitation to proceed.

He leaned forward and gave her a quick peck. Then he kissed her again, longer this time, nibbling very gently on her lower lip.

"I should go," Xin said, standing on the bench.

Jason broke away from Aria and grabbed Xin by the arm. Roughly. "No, stay."

He created a partition in his VR, and drew the two into it with him, giving them some privacy from prying eyes. They appeared on a balcony; it overlooked palm trees and an azure ocean in the distance.

"What's this?" Aria said.

"Something special for the two of you," Jason said. He nodded toward the balcony door. Inside, a king size bed awaited.

Somehow he knew that this was what Xin wanted. And Aria, as well. He realized the knowledge must have been an echo of their previous combining.

Aria smiled vaguely, then grabbed Xin by the hand, and led her inside. The two of them sat on the bed.

"You're so very adorable," Jason told Xin.

"I'm adorable, and she's beautiful, is that it?" Xin said.

"Oh, you're beautiful, don't you worry," Jason said.

"No, I'm not," Xin said. "This isn't even how I really look."

"It doesn't matter," Jason said.

Suddenly she transformed. She was still her, but some imperfections had developed in her features. A few blemishes in her skin. One eye was very slightly smaller than the other. Her lips, not as perfectly formed. But it didn't matter. She was still ravishing, at least to him.

"You *are* beautiful," Jason said. He sat down beside her, and pressed his lips against hers. She mashed her mouth against his, hard.

Finally, he pulled away.

"Massage her," Jason told Xin, his voice shaking slightly.

Xin shyly obeyed, and began to knead the muscles of Aria's back.

Jason in turn massaged Xin. "Your muscles are so stiff. Relax."

"I'm trying," Xin said. "I'm nervous."

"Don't be," Jason said. "Just relax. Let go."

"You act like you've done this before," Xin said.

"Let's just say, I've had my Training AIs run me through a few practice scenarios," Jason told her.

One thing led to another, and soon Jason had them both naked in the bed. One of the fun things about VR was that you weren't limited by your anatomy…

When they were done, Jason lay on his back in the

middle of the king-sized bed, with Xin on his left, and Aria on his right. He had his arms underneath each of their shoulders.

This is the life.

"That was… amazing," Xin said. "At least after I let go of my inhibitions."

"That's what it's all about," Jason said. "Letting go."

"I should have thought of doing something like this a while ago," Aria said.

"What's that?" Jason said.

"Well, I mean, altering my male simulacrums to have multiple, er, extensions," Aria said. "Like you did."

Jason had to smile at that. He'd dismissed those extensions when it was over, but he began to wonder what it would be like to have even more of them. That way he could do more than two girls at the same time.

Hmm, no. Let's not get too greedy.

"How did it feel?" Aria said.

"It's hard to describe," Jason said. "I essentially duplicated the subroutines involved. It wasn't quite double the pleasure, but it was certainly unlike any sexual experience I've ever had."

"Me, as well," Xin said.

Aria kept quiet.

A few moments of silence passed. Then:

"I don't suppose I can get back my company of Bokerov's tanks now?" Aria said.

Jason glanced at her in disbelief, and laughed. "Is that what this was about? You just wanted to jockey for position. For power?"

"Not at all," Aria said. "But I figured I'd ask you now, while you were at your most pliable."

Jason pursed his lips. "I'm still smarting from your previous betrayal…"

"But all that's forgiven now," Aria said sensually. She rubbed a finger across his pectoral muscle, which he had enlarged specifically for this avatar version, along with most of his muscles.

"Is it?" Jason said.

"Yes," Aria said.

Jason shook his head. "Women and their wiles."

Aria shrugged.

"All right, fine," Jason said. He defocused his eyes to call up his HUD, and then he sent Bokerov a message. "Bokerov, I want you to give Aria control of a tank platoon."

"A *company!*" Aria protested.

Jason ignored her. He had to train her to realize that she couldn't get everything she asked for, because if he bowed to her every whim, and those of the other girls, soon he'd have nothing left. Besides, he had to give her something else to work for, to ensure future sexual sessions were as vigorous as this one.

"I've allocated sixteen tanks to your command," Bokerov said. "Feel free to distribute control however you wish."

"Got it, thanks," Jason said. He dismissed Bokerov, and then scrolled through his team on the left side of his HUD. As promised, sixteen Russian tanks had appeared under a "tank company" group. He immediately moved that group underneath Aria, giving her control.

"Thank you," Aria said.

Jason turned toward Xin. "And what do you want from me?"

Xin shrugged. "Nothing." She looked at him, and smiled, which made her cheeks dimple. "I'm happy knowing that I'm wanted the way I am."

Jason was about to tell her that she didn't actually look like that anymore, that her latent self image was nothing like her real world self, but it seemed entirely inappropriate, so he bit his tongue. Especially considering that his own real world self had been nothing to look at, at least when it came to human standards of beauty. Of course, to him, his war machine, and those of the girls, were some of the most beautiful things he'd ever seen. But hey, he was strange like that.

"I can appreciate that," Jason said. He gave her a kiss on the head. "I suppose the two of you have given me what I wanted, too."

"Sex with two real women at once?" Aria said.

"Yes," Jason said. "Though whether or not you're real women is debatable."

"Real female minds, then," Aria said.

"That'll do," Jason said. "Yes, you gave me that. And maybe now, hopefully, you'll show me more loyalty."

Xin pulled away and scowled at him. "Is that why you slept with us? Because you thought it would make us more loyal?"

"Uh, sort of," Jason said. "I mean, I assumed that would be one of the results. But I also like the two of you very much, and—"

Xin slapped him. Her imperfect avatar was replaced with the perfect one once more, and she gave him an imperious look. "I'm never sleeping with you again!"

She vanished.

Jason rubbed his cheek. He had felt the full force of the slap—he had his virtual nerve endings dialed up to max for the sexual romp, and one of the side effects was increased pain sensitivity.

"Well, that didn't quite go as planned," Jason said. He turned toward Aria, who had also shrugged out of his arm. "Can you tell her—"

"You're an asshole," Aria interrupted. She grabbed his crotch and squeezed, hard.

Jason's eyes bulged from the agony, and he quickly dialed down his pain sense.

But then Aria, too, vanished.

Jason threw up his arms. "What the hell did I do?"

He dismissed the virtual partition so that he was back at the picnic table at the lake, sitting there alone.

Lori came walking down the trail that led to the house.

"Hey Babe," Lori sat down beside him on the tabletop and slid an arm over his shoulder.

"Hey," Jason said.

"I was looking for you," Lori said. "But I couldn't find you."

"Oh, I had my AI core in sleep mode," Jason lied.

"Really?" Lori said. "I left a few hooks in place so I could track whether you were asleep or awake, and the hooks told me you were awake, but in another VR partition. I guess the subroutines were malfunctioning."

"Damn it, take those hooks out," Jason said.

Lori shrugged. "So you can lie to me? Okay. It's done."

"How can I be sure you took them out?" Jason said.

"You can't," Lori said. "So I guess that means you'll have to stop lying to me."

Jason sighed. He gazed out across the lake. "I just want to be left alone at the moment."

She still had her arm wrapped around him, and she pulled him closer, squeezing slightly. "We can go to your room, and—"

"I'm not in the mood," Jason said.

"You were just with Tara, weren't you?" Lori said.

"No," Jason said. "I wasn't."

"Oh," Lori said. "Sophie?"

He glanced at Lori. "Look, I—"

"Oh," Lori said. "Xin and Aria, then."

Jason studied her uncertainly. "How did you know I was with the two of them?"

"They swing both ways," Lori said. "It's obvious to anyone who knows what to look for."

"I didn't think that was a requirement for bedding two girls," Jason said.

"It's not," Lori said. "But it helps. Did you get what you wanted out of the transaction?"

"It wasn't a transaction," Jason said. "It was just a release of pent up lust. It won't happen again."

"Oh, I don't mind if it happens again," Lori said. "I just want you to save enough energy for me."

"It's not so much about you minding," Jason said. "It's more that, I pissed them off before they left. I told them I hoped that by making love to them, I'd ensure their loyalty."

"Whoops," Lori said. "Sometimes you suck at this."

"Tell me about it," Jason said.

"It is fixable, though," Lori told him. "Wait a while, maybe a few days. And then tell them you didn't mean what you said. We girls can forgive a lot of things about the men we're attracted to. Also, get approval from Tara this time, please. She's sensitive about things like that. It helps her feel at least some sense of control. Something she needs, if you want to keep her in this relationship."

"I'll do that," Jason said. "Though I'm not sure she'll give me permission."

"You might be surprised at what you can get away with, if you simply ask," Lori said. She gave him a kiss on the cheek, and her eyes became amorous as she pulled away. "That includes me."

Before he could answer, she vanished.

Jason shook his head. "They have to stop doing that."

5

J ason returned to reality shortly after Lori left, and resumed control of his mech from Z.

They walked on through the pine trees for several hours. No attacks came. The Explorer did detect signs of animal habitation: a large swath of trees were trampled and eaten. Jason specifically ordered his army to give such areas a wide berth. He didn't want to encounter any fauna, at least until his units were back up to par.

There was only so much that could be repaired without actual ore, and polycarbonate. Jason ordered the troops to try digging into the ground at one point, but the bedrock in this particular area didn't have much metallic content, so Jason had to order some of the more damaged units in Bokerov's army to be disman-tled for parts and materials. Those machines, when they went offline, were dragged along by other units until nothing remained of them, so that the army didn't have to halt its advance. Incidentally, Jason also replaced his railgun slugs using metal retrieved from those units.

As repairs were made, Jason instructed the drones that were freed up to concentrate on fixing the more severely damaged units. Eventually, all of the mechs and their clones were repaired, along with most members of Bokerov's army, save for the Cataphracts. At that point, Jason directed all repair units to swarm about them to accelerate the process; he had to sacrifice two full tanks to repair the damage the units had suffered. The cost was worth it, however, because Jason judged a fully functioning Cataphract worth ten times more than a fully functioning tank. They had lost the Torch, Dinosaur, and Horse before traveling through the rift, but that still left seven Cataphracts Jason could utilize in coming battles.

When the remaining units in the army were finally repaired, Jason could rest a little easier. So far they hadn't been attacked, but he had little doubt the current pristine state of affairs would last for long. Sure enough, only a couple of hours after the last Cataphract was repaired, they had their first encounter with the native wildlife.

The Explorer passed over a ridge, and sighted a herd of large, giraffe-like creatures eating the lichen-like leaves on the pine trees. The creatures essentially looked like hippopotamuses, from head to tail, except for their humongous size, and the massive necks that allowed them to reach the tops of the trees.

Jason shared the Explorer feed with the rest of his army.

"We should call them Stretchy Hippos!" Lori said.

"That's lame," Sophie said. "Girahips. That's what I'm calling them."

"I love it!" Lori said.

"Er, on second thought," Sophie said.

"We'll go with Girahips," Jason said. "But in any case, it looks like we're going to have to take another detour. I don't want to get close to these animals."

"Why not?" Lori said. "They look like harmless plant eaters!"

"But look how huge they are," Iris said. "Even plant eaters can be deadly if you disturb them. I agree with Jason. We don't want to disturb these creatures."

Jason turned the army to the west, or what he was calling west, anyway, and they marched through the tall pine trees, intending to give the creatures a wide berth.

Jason felt the ground vibrating underneath him.

"Uh, does anyone else feel that?" Maeran asked.

"Yes," Cheyanne said. She took to the air, and flew above the treetops.

The Rex Wolves began barking wildly, their bodies positioned northward.

Jason had directed the Explorer west with the team, but he rotated the scout to the north, toward the herd. The Girahips were running toward them. A large one, probably the equivalent of a bull, led the charge. Racing directly toward Jason and his army.

"They're coming directly at us!" Cheyanne said.

"Something must have spooked them," Tara said.

"But what?" Jason said. "I can't see anything…"

"Obviously, they're smaller than the trees them-selves," Jerry said.

"Turn south!" Jason said. "Try to get out of the path of these Girahips." He was already racing south before he finished speaking, and weaved between the different pines. The other War Forgers and their clones followed him. The tanks began to shift positions as well, but moved more slowly than the mechs.

The Rex Wolves followed alongside the main War Forgers. They moved at speed, tails strung out behind them, well aware of the coming danger.

"At the rate those Girahips are incoming, there's no way the tanks will move out of the way in time," Tara said. "We might, but the rest of the army will be over-run. And they'll have to face whatever is chasing them."

"Then we'll fight!" Jason said, still weaving west.

"Oh goodie," Bokerov said. "We get to kill again!"

"You really like killing, don't you?" John said.

"When it comes to killing versions of you, yes," Bokerov said. "But killing anything else comes a close second. Especially when that something else is an organic. Mm, organics. So soft and squishy."

"You know, sometimes I think this Bokerov dude is actually sane," Aria said. "Other times, that he's bat shit crazy."

"Definitely bat shit," Tara 5 said. "You have no idea what he did to us in his VR dungeon."

"Imagine enduring that for months on end," Iris said.

"Oh, we did," Tara 5 said. "At least it seemed like it. He adjusted our time sense to the slowest possible level."

"What can I say, I'm a sick, perverted individual," Bokerov said. "This is what happens when you have your mind trapped inside a machine for sixty years."

"Great," John said. "Something to look forward to, sixty years from now. We all become Bokerovs."

"No," Jason said, squeezing between two tight trees. "We won't. We're not like him."

"Oh, but you are," Bokerov said. "You'll see." He giggled softly.

And then a huge Girahip bull came trampling through the trees beside Jason. He switched to Bullet Time, and attempted to dodge out of the way, but the creature was moving too fast, and plowed right into him. Jason was flung to the side and smashed into a pine tree; he bounced off and used his accelerated time sense to land on his feet.

"Damn things move almost as fast as us!" Tara said.

"Not as fast as the combat robots I used to have!" Bokerov said. At the periphery of Jason's vision, on the far side of the army, Bokerov was opening fire with several of his tanks, ripping into the Girahips that were smashing through the trees there.

"Why are you firing?" Jason said. "I didn't give the order!" He dodged another Girahip that nearly plowed into him.

"I'm only trying to steer them away from my tanks," Bokerov said.

"Well, it's not working." Jason watched as several Girahips trampled his tanks; the units held up well under the sudden compressive pressure however.

Another solid wall of Girahips came at him. They

squeezed between the trees, and some even crashed right into those trees to get away from whatever was chasing them.

Jason and the others dodged the Girahips as well as they were able, but some of them were inevitably trampled, like Bokerov's tanks.

Tara fired her grappling hook at the neck of one Girahips, and then pulled herself onto its back as it steered her away.

"Ride them, if you can!" Tara said.

Jason switched to a run, and darted south through the trees, following alongside one of the Girahips. He managed to wrap his arms around the neck, but when he tried to pull himself up, he succeeded only in yanking the Girahip toward the ground. The animal crashed, and then flung Jason away before scrambling to its feet and dashing off.

Jason was struck by another Girahip as he got up, and the creature gored his mech with the small pair of horns on its head.

Jason arose, and then Tara was at his side, shoving him out of the path of another Girahip.

"Thought you were riding them?" Jason said.

"I was," Tara said. "But the damn thing couldn't support my weight, and crumpled after only a short distance."

"So much for that idea," Jason said.

Sophie landed nearby, as did Aria. The latter deployed her ballistic shield, and used it to deflect incoming Girahips, herding them away from Jason and the other two.

He glanced at his overhead map, and confirmed where the other members of his team were located. The Girahips had separated them. Lori was the closest, at forty meters away.

And then Jason saw what was chasing the Girahips.

From the trees came a beast unlike anything that had come before. This one had the body of a cheetah, though ten times the size, and its head was that of a monitor lizard, replete with forked tongue. Oh, and it had two deadly rows of teeth framing its mouth. It wasn't as tall as the trees, which explained why it wasn't visible by the Explorer from afar.

"Well, that looks friendly," Tara said.

The creature was intent on chasing the Girahip in front of it, but when it saw Aria, it immediately spun toward her, perhaps believing her easier prey.

Invisible plasma bolts fired from beside Aria, plowing into the creature, and it faltered, roaring angrily. Jason realized Lori had approached in secret, her invisibility mode active.

It leaped on Aria, and attempted to chew into her shield.

"*Now* we can fire!" Jason said. "At will!"

Sophie unleashed her micro machines, drilling into the attacker's side. Aria fired her lightning bolt weapon over the tip of her shield.

Jason was about to launch his energy weapon, when Tara blocked his sight line, and stabbed the beast with her sword. The combination of their attacks felled the creature.

Another of similar size came up behind it. This one

paused to swallow a nearby boulder whole, then it turned toward the party, and breathed a stream of super-heated slugs.

Aria narrowly directed her shield toward the attack in time. Some of the blows were deflected, but the rest embedded in the ballistic shield, thanks to their super-heated nature.

"Did it just eat that boulder and convert them into slugs, becoming an organic railgun?" Tara said.

"Apparently," Aria said. "But I don't think the thing realizes it's only reinforcing my shield by doing that."

"Dragon Cheetah!" Lori said. She fired her plasma bolt at the beast and it dodged to the side.

"What's that?" Jason said.

"Their name!" Lori said. "I'm calling them Dragon Cheetahs! I named them first this time! So we use my name!'

"All right," Jason said. Three Dragon Cheetahs barreled through the trees. "I'm not really worried about what we call them right now." He unleashed his energy weapon at one, and the girls took down the other two. But then another Dragon Cheetah was leaping on him from the trees. It struck his armor, and those huge, sickle-shaped talons tore big gashes into his hull.

Tara came at him, and stabbed her sword into its rib cage. The Dragon Cheetah howled, and swept its claw at her, swiping her aside. Aria fired her lightning bolt weapon into the wound, and that finished the beast off.

Five more came through the trees.

The Rex Wolves burst through the foliage and inter-cepted. Bruiser clamped down on the neck of his target, and pinned it. The other three meanwhile scrapped, wrestling with their foes. Jason aimed at the one that was fighting Shaggy, and increased his time sense to ensure his shot didn't miss. He fired, and the Dragon Cheetah went limp.

Lori similarly helped Runt, while Tara fired her laser at the creature that held Lackey.

"They keep coming!" Xin said from where she was fighting nearby. "This is some kind of super pack!"

"They definitely like to track in huge packs," Jerry agreed.

"Combining might be order," Aria said.

"I wouldn't recommend it," Bokerov said. "Look at my Cataphracts."

Jason rotated his Explorer feed during a break in the fighting, and spotted the Cataphracts towering over the trees to the south. Because of their height, protruding above the treetops, they served as a beacon for the Dragon Cheetahs, and they seemed to be drawing in the majority of them. The creatures swarmed about them, overwhelming their hulls. Their weapons were unable to keep up. Bokerov had resorted to shooting at them with his nearby tanks to try to get them off. The Dragon Cheetahs were repeatedly biting into the hulls, taking out big chunks of metal.

They attacked other tanks nearby, too. Sometimes they swallowed nearby rocks and boulders, and breathed those super-heated slugs in attack. And their teeth and claws could easily cut through a hull, peeling it open. Not that they'd find anything edible inside any of their units but AI cores.

"I think these Tyrnari must have trained them," Tara said as she cut off another head.

"What do you mean?" Jason fired his energy weapon as a Dragon Cheetah came at him. The head exploded.

"There's nothing of nutritional value inside any of our machines," Tara said. "But that's not stopping them from checking each and every one, as if they expect to find a juicy prize inside. If the Tyrnari have dispatched any of their Phaser mechs or equivalents out here, with organic pilots inside, that would explain the irrational behavior."

"Maybe," Aria said. "Or perhaps they just like to rip open anything that moves."

"That could be it, too," Tara admitted.

Aria had apparently called up her platoon of tanks, because eight of them arrived, and arranged in a half circle beside her to launch plasma bolts into the Dragon Cheetahs.

Beside Jason, Shaggy fought at his side. Runt stayed near Lori, and Bruiser and Lackey with Tara.

Jason was running low on power, so he scooped up the body of a dead Dragon Cheetah, and used it as a club. This had been a favorite tactic of his when dealing with bioweapons back on Earth, and it worked well enough now.

Maybe not: after bashing in the head of one of the Dragon Cheetahs, when he swung at the next one, the creature dodged the blow and snapped at the corpse, latching on. The beast tugged, hard, and managed to pull it out of his grip.

"Shit." Jason leaped back as the Dragon Cheetah came at him, swaying its head back and forth to swing the dead corpse around like some oversized fish.

Iris landed at his side, and her six legged mech began vibrating the ground. She lashed out with her energy whips, cutting deep gashes into the corpse, but not enough to cut through it. She lowered the intensity of the weapons, and wrapped the whips around the corpse, and then yanked, ripping the body away from the Dragon Cheetah.

It had apparently downed a boulder at some point, because it unleashed a stream of super-heated slugs at Jason and Iris.

Maeran landed beside them, and sent her drones in front of the attack. They formed a triangular shape, and the energy beam shared between them deflected the slugs; when the blast ended, she amped up the power output so that the energy beams became cutting, and then launched her drones toward the Dragon Cheetah.

The big creature dodged to the side; Maeran spat that gooey substance from her mouth, and caught one of the Dragon Cheetah's feet. It struggled to break free as the drones swooped in, but could not; a moment later the drones had separated its head from its body.

Three more Dragon Cheetahs came crashing through the trees.

Shaggy intercepted one, rolling to the ground with it.

Cheyanne dove down from above, slicing off the heads of the other two creatures with her swords.

Then she darted upward, and weaved in and out

between the other attackers, striking surgically as she did so.

Two Dragon Cheetahs leaped upward, each grabbing onto one of Cheyanne's legs with their jaws. They bit down hard, and it looked like they were going to tear the legs right off. Cheyanne fell because of the added weight, but before she hit the ground, she activated her shockwave weapon, and the energy wave struck the creatures, sending them flying backward with blood oozing from their orifices. Cheyanne took flight once more, those dragonfly-like wings a blur.

"Get back!" Iris anchored her six legs, and began pounding the ground with the thicker bottom portions. She was able to direct the vibrations forward, away from Jason and the others, and destabilized the ground underneath the incoming Dragon Cheetahs, sending them off balance. That made them easy prey for Sophie's micro machines, and Cheyanne's swords.

The bodies of the dead Dragon Cheetahs piled up, and finally the attackers broke. One of those in the back saw what was happening, and raised his head to issue a resounding, well, screech was the best way to describe it. In moments, the entire herd had turned back and was retreating through the trees so that just as fast as the attack had begun, it ended.

Iris ceased her vibrating attack.

Jason surveyed the felled trees, and countless corpses around him. He checked his overhead map, and ran a quick inventory on the surviving units.

All of the War Forgers and their clones had survived, albeit with several damaged parts. Bokerov had lost five tanks, and three artillery units. All of his Cataphracts had survived.

"Deploy the repair drones," Jason said. "Let's fix what we can. Use the fallen tanks and artillery units for spare parts if you need them."

Jason's drones deployed, and began repairing the gashes in his chest.

Aria walked up to one of the corpses.

"Look at this," she said, turning the body over with a kick. The torso was split right open, giving Jason a grotesque view of its chest cavity. "They all have two sets of lungs, like our Rex Wolves. I'm guessing this world was terraformed at one point, to create the bioweapons the empire demands of its member systems. As was almost done to Earth."

"Well, looks like they're biologically compatible with the mutated bioweapons from our own world," Xin said, nodding at the Rex Wolves, who were feasting on one dead Dragon Cheetah each.

"We'll see," Lori said. "If they throw up a few minutes from now, we'll know for sure."

But the Rex Wolves didn't throw up.

"A world that has been terraformed to create bioweapons," Jason said. He shook his head. "The Banthar invaded sixty years ago because they wanted to turn Earth into a breeding ground for bioweapons. But the Tyrnari already beat them to this world, it looks like."

"It could be the equivalent of an intergalactic arms race, as different alien races vie for favor in this empire of theirs," Cheyanne said. "Destroying as many worlds as they can to create the bioweapons for the empire's wars."

"Interesting idea," Xin said.

Aria's avatar appeared, nodding. "This world had to have been invaded at some point. There's no other way to explain the compatible atmosphere our own mutants are experiencing, nor the apparent tissue digestibility."

Iris picked up one of the bodies in her four hands, and a yellow mist emerged from gills in its side.

"Did you see that mist coming out of the gills?" Iris said. "They're contributing to the atmospheric contents. Just like typical Earth bioweapons."

"When my War Forgers were taking down some of those large, rectangular airships back on Earth, we discovered bioweapons that were similar to these," Julian said. "They escaped the wreckages of the airships, and swarmed onto the plains, running away."

"So if the Tyrnari invaders are successful, this is the future of Earth we're looking at here," Jason said.

"And it's certainly not pretty," Aria added.

6

Jason returned to VR while waiting for the repair drones to fix the damage to his army. Several tanks had damaged treads as a consequence of bearing the crushing weight of the bioweapons that had stomped over them, and as such the army was immobile until further notice. He considered simply dragging those tanks along via other units, but decided their advance would be faster if they concentrated on repairing the treads, first. He put Z in charge of his mech, and she promised to notify him if there was anything amiss in the real world.

He'd created a duplicate of his VR environment, and activated the copy in a separate partition, because he wasn't in the mood for talking with any of the girls tonight.

He was jogging on the path around the lake, and he planned to do a climb afterwards. Maybe he'd get in some skiing after that—he'd developed a liking for the sport, ever since Lori had introduced him to it. He'd gotten good quickly: gotta love being a machine.

He sighed, just enjoying everything about his life. Sure, he was trapped on an alien world, probably hundreds of light years away from Earth, but he had such a rich inner world, courtesy of VR. Where else could he have a whole mountain trail to himself for jogging purposes, except here? Or an entire gaggle of beautiful women begging to sleep with him?

Well, they weren't exactly begging at the moment, but hey, part of that was his own doing. And not just because he had partitioned his VR.

Two girls were mad at him. A third would be as well when she found out what he'd done. So far, only one girl was truly constant, someone he could rely upon without fail to accept him, despite all his faults and mistakes. Why couldn't they all be like Lori?

I really have to take some proper time to manage my harem, if I want this to work.

He received a call from Tara.

He hesitated to answer it, at first. He had hoped to put off the discussion he needed to have with her, but he decided he might as well get it over with. She'd hate his guts when he was done, and it would be sad that he would never be able to hold her in his arms again, but he supposed he could always construct a virtual reality simulacrum in her image if he really wanted to.

He accepted. "Hey," he said, voice only.

"Hey back," Tara said. "Can I get an invite to your VR partition? Unless you're *occupied*."

The way she said the last word told him she was suggesting he might be with another woman.

"No, I'm not occupied," Jason said. He paused his run, and took a moment to catch his breath. It didn't take long—he just reset his simulated cardiopulmonary system.

He gave her an invite and Tara appeared in front of him on the trail.

She wore her diaphanous white dress today, open all the way down the middle to her belly button, revealing the sides of her breasts. Her hair was in a long pony-tail that reached to the small of her back. She wore a lei of flowers, as per her Hawaiian heritage. Well, Polynesian to be exact. She also had a flower in her hair today, which only added to her beauty.

"I sometimes forget how easy on the eyes you are," Jason said.

She smiled, seeming slightly sad. "You tell that to all the girls, don't you?"

"Not at all," Jason said. "I've only ever said those words to you."

"Ah," Tara told him. "So then you admit you've said variants to the others, calling them beautiful, just not in so many words."

Jason sighed. "I suppose so."

"I'm not so special anymore, am I?" Tara said. "I liked it when it was just me and Lori who were sharing your bed. When the two of us were all you knew in the sexual department."

"You're still special," Jason said.

"No, I'm just a fuck," Tara said.

"That's not true," Jason said. "Don't even talk like that."

She shrugged. "Well, it's what I wanted in the beginning anyway, if you recall. I promised you we wouldn't have to have a relationship. That it would be just for fun. Well I got my wish, I suppose. Ever heard the saying, careful what you wish for? I should have been very careful, yes."

Jason didn't know what to say to that. So instead, he decided to change the subject. It was time to steer the conversation down the path he had been dreading.

"I have to tell you something." Jason couldn't help the sudden nervous edge to his voice.

Tara looked up. Her shoulders tensed. There was fear in her eyes.

"I, well…" Jason couldn't meet her eyes. Then he blurted it out all at once. "I slept with Aria and Xin. I forgot to ask for permission. I know you wanted that, but I figured, there wouldn't be any harm in it, because I'm probably not going to do it again, and—"

He realized he was rambling, and when he looked at her, he saw that she seemed relieved. Her shoulders had relaxed, and she slumped slightly as he watched.

"Is that it?" Tara said. "I thought you were going to tell me you were breaking up with me or something."

"No, not at all," Jason said.

"Well good," Tara said. "So then. Yes, it's okay. You have my permission to fuck Aria and Xin. And Sophie as well. And the new girls, too, if you want."

"Why the sudden openness?" Jason asked.

"Just seems easier this way," Tara said. "To give you

permission ahead of time, and all. Less angst for all parties involved."

Jason was at a loss for words.

"I just want you to be happy," Tara explained into the silence.

Finally Jason found his voice. "I *am* happy. I was happy with you and Lori alone. But I just, lost my way, I guess. The temptation… the girls, well, they were just throwing themselves at me for a while there. I didn't know what to do. I figured, why not?"

She smiled sadly. "You don't need to explain yourself. Look, when I say I want you to be happy, I've realized now that your happiness is directly linked to the well-being of the girls. When they're happy and content, it translates into behavior that makes you happy and content. Look at what happened with Aria and Xin at the rift. How they attacked you. I bet they won't do that ever again, not after you fucked them."

"We'll see," Jason said.

"No, it's true," Tara said. "Having sex with someone releases dopamine. It forms a bond."

"In humans, maybe," Jason said.

"In us, too," Tara said. "Our subroutines are written to mimic dopamine down to the binary level. You've bonded with them, along with the rest of us. They'll be loyal."

"Well sure, but I made the mistake of actually telling them that," Jason said.

Tara tapped her lips in thought. "What did you tell them, exactly?"

"Well, let's see," Jason said. "After we all climaxed, and were lying in bed together—"

"Uh, thanks for that," Tara said. "Unnecessary details!"

"Uh, sorry," Jason said. "Anyway, I told them that maybe now, hopefully, they'd show me more loyalty."

"Ah," Tara said. "While that might have been the point of the transaction, it's best not to tell women something like that outright."

"Yeah, I figured that," Jason said.

"Why did you call it a transaction?" Jason said. "That's what Lori calls it, too, when I do it with someone else."

"We talked about this, Lori and I," Tara said. "When you have sex with someone else, it's simply a transaction. When you have sex with us, it's lovemaking. It's how we rationalize sharing you. Otherwise, I don't think we could handle the jealousy."

"Ah," Jason said.

She sat down on a small rock next to the lake, and gazed out at the towering cliff face that was reflected upon the smooth surface in front of her.

"There's something I wanted to tell you," Tara said.

"What, you're pregnant?" Jason joked.

She gave him a hurt look, and Jason quickly wiped the grin off his face. He took a seat on a rock beside her.

"So what is it?" he pressed.

She looked at his face searchingly. Her eyes were suddenly sad again. "Why is this so hard?"

"What?" Jason said.

She swallowed visibly. "Well." She looked away. "Come on, silly Tara, just tell him." She finally met his eyes again. "I've, well, ever since we met on the irradiated plains that day, there's been something between us."

"Yes, a tension," Jason said. "Sexual, I guess."

"That, and something more," Tara said.

"What do you mean?"

"Just that," Tara said. "I… well." She looked down. "I… really like you."

"Oh, I like you, too," Jason said, maybe a bit too quickly. Almost like a brush off.

She squeezed her hands together, tightly, apparently not pleased at his tone. When she spoke, her voice was soft, as if she was talking more to herself than him. "I couldn't tell you. I tried when the moment came, but I couldn't do it."

"Tell me *what?*" Jason pressed.

She sighed, and her fingers relaxed. She looked into his eyes once more. "Just fuck me, please."

She draped her body backward over the small rock, and Jason used the VR build tools to elongate the gray edges to support her. He enlarged the rock to hold himself as well.

Instead of vanishing his clothes, he purposely undressed, and then did the same with her.

After the sex, she promptly sat up and pulled on her clothes.

"Well, I won't keep you," Tara said.

"Wait," Jason said. "At least snuggle a bit or something."

"Aw, that's sweet," Tara said. "But unnecessary. I don't need to snuggle."

"But if you leave right now, it'll just make me feel used," Jason said.

Tara shrugged. "I thought that's what you guys like?"

"No," Jason said.

"I once met a man who asked me, what was the longest time in the world?" Tara said. "I told him I had no idea. Then he explained that the longest time in the world was the time between his climax, and when the woman left. So. I don't want to prolong your torture more than it needs to be."

And with that, she vanished.

Jason shook his head. *Damn it. I'll never understand her!*

Once again he was wishing all the girls were like Lori.

Unfortunately, his day wasn't done yet. He had to set things right with Aria and Xin. Given that Aria had protected him in the last battle, he suspected things were probably okay with her, but he needed to check. As for Xin, well, he'd find out shortly, he supposed.

He planned to make this quick.

He returned to his standard VR partition, and checked if Aria and Xin were logged in. They were, surprisingly. He was ready to request an invite to their private VRs, but now he didn't have to worry about that. They were located relatively close together, as expected.

He teleported to their location, deep in the woods next to the lake.

They were chopping wood together. They'd felled at least three trees with axes, and were currently splitting smaller logs on the severed trucks.

Jason approached.

Aria looked up, but Xin ignored him.

"Hey," Jason said.

Aria returned her attention to the task at hand.

"What are you doing?" Jason said.

"Making a dojo," Aria said. "So we can practice sparring."

"Why does it look like you're making firewood, then?" Jason asked.

Neither answered.

"What's the point of a dojo?" Jason said. "It won't translate into the real world."

"But it could," Aria said. "We could spar in virtual mechs, too, not just human forms."

Jason cocked his head. "Why build it by hand instead of using VR tools?"

"Distracts our minds," Xin said.

"From what?" Jason said.

"From our situation here, trapped on this planet," Aria said. A moment later she added: "And from you."

"Ah," Jason said. "You're still pissed at me."

Aria threw her ax away and stalked toward him. "You're damn straight we're pissed. You have a lot of nerve showing up here." Her anger seemed a bit forced. Theatrical. Especially considering they had fought together against bioweapons only a short time ago. But Jason decided to let her have her little show of outrage. He'd take it like a man.

He only worried that it wouldn't make a difference.

He saw Xin watching the confrontation from the corner of her eye, judging him.

"You slept with us because you wanted to secure our loyalty," Aria said. "Not because you're attracted to us. And that's the worst possible thing a man can ever do to a woman. Well, other than loving someone else."

"That's not true," Jason said. "I slept with you because I was attracted. But I guess I was also thinking strategically, too. I can't help it. I lead an army now."

She didn't answer.

"Let me make it up to you," Jason said.

"How?" Aria said.

"I'll give you that company of tanks," Jason said.

Aria turned away. "I don't want it anymore."

She fetched her ax, and returned to the stump.

"What do you want?" Jason asked.

"For starters," Aria said. "Some respect. Don't treat us like property."

"I never did," Jason said.

"If you say so," Aria said. She struck down at the wood she'd placed on the trunk, and split it in half.

"What about you, Xin?" Jason said. "How can I show you that you're more to me than just some piece on a 3D chess board?"

"No need," Xin said. "I will forgive you in my own time. I just need space. What you're doing here, it comes off as needy. It's not like you."

"I guess... I don't want to lose either of you," Jason said.

"Because we're valuable members of your team?"

Aria said. "Or because you want to use us, to protect you."

"The former," Jason said.

Aria nodded. "I believe you."

"Xin?" Jason said.

"As I told you, I need time," Xin said. "But for what it's worth, I believe you, as well."

"Thank you," Jason said. "I'd offer to help build this dojo of yours, but I have a feeling I'm not wanted at the moment."

"You'd be correct in that regard," Xin said.

Jason sighed gently, and then logged out of his VR.

Sometimes, the real world was better than the virtual.

7

W hen the treads of the damaged tanks were repaired enough to move on, Jason gave the order to proceed north once more. Repairs continued on the other units in the meantime, and as usual, the army dragged the wreckages of the completely destroyed units along for spare parts.

They used the path the Girahips had trampled through the forest. The units had to step over and around the dead bodies of the Dragon Cheetahs that clogged the immediate area, but as soon the army left those bodies behind, the units were able to advance without impediments.

They soon reached the area where the Girahips had been trimming the pine trees with their jaws, and then passed it, continuing through the tall trees, northward.

The repairs were completed in a couple of hours. Jason glanced at the sky, and realized that the sun hadn't moved from its position.

"I wonder if the sun ever sets here," Tara commented, giving voice to his thoughts.

"That can be both good, and bad," Jason said.

"Good, because it means we'll always be able to see where we're going," Lori said. "Bad, because so will the alien bioweapons."

"We can see with LIDAR," Aria said. "So we don't need sunlight."

"I was thinking more along the lines of, it's good, because our power cells will always be recharging," Jason said.

"Ah!" Lori said. "I knew that!"

"Then why didn't you say it?" Sophie asked.

"Dunno, slipped my mind!" Lori replied.

"You're a machine now," Xin said. "Nothing can actually 'slip your mind,' as you say."

"Nuh-uh," Lori said. "Trust me, things slip my mind all the time!"

"I actually believe her on that," Sophie said. The condescension in her voice was obvious.

Iris came alongside Jason's mech. She switched to a private channel. Her avatar appeared.

"Interesting team you have here," the Middle Eastern woman said. "Tell me, how do you keep them together? Are you sleeping with them?"

"Well, that's none of your business, is it?" Jason said.

"Actually, it is," Iris said. "I'm part of this team now, too. I have to know what to expect."

"I don't think I'll be sleeping with you, if that's what you're getting at," Jason said. "I have my hands full already. Trust me. I don't think the girls would like it.

You ask how I keep them together? By not getting romantically involved with anyone." It was such a blatant lie, he thought she wasn't going to believe him.

But she nodded her head anyway. "Interesting."

Jason wasn't sure why he'd lied to her. He supposed it was because he wanted to dispel any notions she might have had about sleeping with him. Best to get such thoughts out of her head early on. Otherwise the walking disaster that his own team had become would only worsen.

"I lived in Little Persia, in New York," Iris said. "The biggest concentration of Persians in the world, considering that we lost our homeland to the invaders. We are actually very liberal. I used to attend what we called 'slumber parties.' Essentially a euphemism for orgies."

"You went to orgies?" Jason said. There was only a hint of disbelief in his voice. He wasn't surprised by anything anymore.

"Yes," Iris said. "It was interesting, though the experience was entirely empty. Devoid of emotion. It was like having sex while your mind is constrained by Containment Code, and without emotions. Something we did often with Bokerov. The lust and pleasure are still there, but no emotional satisfaction whatsoever."

"Doesn't sound very fun," Jason said.

"No," Iris said. "Now that I have emotions back again, I'm hopeful that one day, I'll be able to have some sort of relationship with another human being. Or I suppose, the only relationship I can have these days is with a Mind Refurb, such as yourself."

"Yeah, but as I said, I don't get romantically involved," Jason said.

"Lori tells me otherwise," Iris said.

Jason nearly threw up his arms.

Damn it, she blabs to everyone.

"It's all right if you don't want me," Iris said. "I can try my luck with your other clones."

Jason sighed. "It's not that I don't want you, it's just that I have my hands full managing the girls as it is. And trust me, my other clones will be just as preoccupied. There's just no room for anyone else."

"I understand," Iris said. "So we're good for a date tonight at 8 P.M., Standard Time? I will cook *Baqala polow* for you."

"Uh, I just said there's no room for anyone else?" Jason said.

"Great, see you in your VR at 8," Iris said. Her avatar winked out, and she decreased her pace so that she was no longer walking alongside him.

They just don't give up.

Well, he had to admire her persistence. He planned to avoid his VR tonight at 8, however.

An alert sounded on his HUD. His Explorer had spotted something.

Jason switched his attention to the remote feed. There were white, elliptical flyers approaching. The kind the Tyrnari favored.

"Well, we've got company," Jason said.

He recalled the Explorer and landed it on a treetop nearby. The drone balanced delicately on the upper branches.

"Bokerov, ready to do some killing?" Jason said.

"Always am," Bokerov said.

"Defensive positions, War Forgers," Jason said.

The different team members and their clones aimed their weapons at the sky above the tree line ahead, and waited. Sophie used her jumpjets to land on the upper branch of a nearby tree, while Cheyanne did the same with her wings.

Bokerov, meanwhile, ordered his Cataphracts to lie down, so that their upper bodies would be hidden by the trees.

"You know, the Cataphracts were probably already sighted," Aria said. "It's why the Tyrnari are headed our way."

"She's right," Jones said. "We already agreed those things can be spotted for kilometers around."

"Yes, but Bokerov is going to reposition them," Jason said. "So that when they reemerge, their new locations will be a surprise. Isn't that right, Bokerov?"

"I'll reposition them as well as I'm able," Bokerov said. "The bipedals will have to low crawl, which is a tricky thing for a Cataphract, as you call it, to do. Some of the quadrupeds will have difficulty as well, due to the nature of their limbs. The Sphinx, for example, can only move very slowly in a crawl position."

"Do what you can," Jason said.

He glanced at the overhead map and watched as the flyers approached. Their red dots updated, courtesy of the Explorer which kept them in sight at all times.

The incoming red dots suddenly froze.

For a moment Jason thought the Explorer had been

destroyed, or ceased transmitting in some way, but the signal was good. He glanced at the video feed and confirmed the elliptical shapes weren't moving.

"What the hell are they up to..." Jason said.

Tense moments ticked past.

"They must be waiting for reinforcements," Tara said. "They've detected the trap we've laid for them, and don't want to spring it just yet. We should attack now, before any further reinforcements arrive."

"I'm detecting a transmission," Aria said.

Jason realized he was receiving something on an open channel as well.

"They're using a human comm channel," Sophie said.

"They would have learned the protocol from Bokerov," Maeran said. "Along with our languages."

"This is true," Bokerov said. "Once they were able to reverse engineer our protocols, I shared my entire language database with them. This was over ten years ago. They've had plenty of time to learn Russian, and other languages, since then."

Jason overlaid the audio and video from that particular comm channel over his main channel, and played back the voice-only message his AI core had already recorded.

"Human troops," a deep male voice said. "I am Jhagan. Servant of Risilan, of the Modlenth Branch. I wish to speak with your leader."

"It has to be a trick," Tara said. "A delaying tactic, meant to make us wait here for their reinforcements."

"She's right," Bokerov said. "We must attack, immediately! Let me unleash my cannons!"

Jason reached toward his face, and tried to rub his chin before he realized he didn't have one anymore. He made up his mind.

"I want to hear what they have to say," Jason said.

He signed into the comm channel the aliens were using, and spoke. "I'm Jason. Leader of the War Forgers. This is my army. And we're three seconds away from blasting you out of the skies. So tell me what you want, and make it quick."

"The Central wishes to see you," Jhagan returned.

"Who?" Jason said.

"Risilan, of the Modlenth Branch," Jhagan said.

"That means nothing to me," Jason said.

"Risilan is our leader," Jhagan said. "The Central."

"Oh," Jason said. "Modlenth Branch. You're some kind of Tyrnari faction?"

"That is correct," Jhagan said.

"And you're not allied with the faction invading Earth?" Jason pressed.

"Also correct," Jhagan replied.

"What does your Central want with us?" Jason said.

"I'm afraid only she can reveal that information to you," Jhagan said. "In person. I am here to escort you."

Jason muted the line.

"This could be the break we've been looking for," Jason said. "This faction might be able to help us defeat the invading Tyrnari."

"Or it could be a trick," Tara said.

"It must be," Bokerov said. "Let's shoot them down."

"I think we should at least meet this Risilan," Jerry said.

"I agree," Jones said.

"I know you're probably discussing this news amongst yourselves, in an attempt to come to a decision on whether or not to join us," Jhagan said. "But I urge you, decide quickly. The Imperials signaled for reinforcements before the last of their army entered the rift. We beat these reinforcements to you, but I'm afraid we only have a few minutes until they arrive."

Jason decided to take a chance. "We'll go with him."

"What, no vote?" Sophie said.

"This isn't a democracy," Jason said. He unmuted the line. "We'll go with you to meet this Central. Lead the way."

He turned toward Aria and Xin. "This time, try not to attack them, please."

Xin shrugged. "Like you said, this isn't a democracy."

"What's that supposed to mean?" Jason asked.

"Figure it out," Xin told him.

"Such disrespect!" Bokerov said. "Dominate them!"

"I think she means she might attack them if she wants!" Lori said.

"Yeah, I got that," Jason said.

He sent Xin a private message. "You can't make comments like that over the public comm. If you want to disagree with an order, I have to ask that you do it in private. This sets a bad precedent for the rest of the team."

"I'm sorry," Xin said. "I guess I'm still a little angry about your loyalty comment. I think perhaps I will lower my emotion settings for the time being."

"Probably a good idea," Jason said. "So you're going to keep flippant comments to yourself? Or ping me directly if you have something you disagree with?"

"Yes," Xin said.

"Can I get your word that you're not going to attack these Tyrnari?" Jason said.

"You have my word," Xin said. "As I mentioned, I was simply letting my emotions run wild. It won't happen again, I promise you."

"Thank you," Jason said.

On the Explorer feed, the elliptical flyers moved forward until they were visible above the tree line overhead.

The lichen-covered undergrowth ahead shuddered as robots emerged. Stepping forward, they had two legs for walking, but four grasping arms. Otherwise, they were mostly humanoid in shape.

Jason and the others immediately trained their weapons on the new arrivals.

"They are with me," Jhagan said. "They are part of your escort. Quickly, the Imperials are almost here."

Some of the new mechs dashed to the east, following the direction the flyers were heading over-head. Some stayed behind, as if waiting for Jason and the others to move. These mechs were roughly half as tall as those of Jason and the girls. Jason called them 'mechs' because of their size, but they could have been pure robots—there was no evidence they harbored pilots inside.

There were also no signs of servomotors or other machine components: like the Phaser mechs, their bodies were covered in a metal skin that was smooth, almost organic-like. A small area in the chest region emitted a silvery glow, while the rest of the exterior was a light, metallic blue. There was no sign of any weaponry anywhere on those bodies, but if they were anything like the Phaser mechs of the other Tyrnari, these machines harbored their weapons hidden inside their many forearms.

The Rex Wolves growled at the lingering units.

"Easy, boys," Tara said. She grabbed Bruiser by the scruff of the neck when the animal lurched forward. At the same time, she patted Lackey on the neck with her other hand, ready to similarly restrain the animal.

"All right, we head east," Jason said.

Xin led the way, to show the others that she had no intention of attacking. Aria followed, along with Jason and the rest. As he weaved between the trees and trampled the undergrowth, Jason launched his Explorer, sending it into the air next to the flyers.

As usual, the tanks were the slowest moving in the bunch, and the War Forgers and their clones easily passed them by. The Cataphracts followed behind them, having risen so that their top sections protruded from the forest once more.

The mechs that had lingered behind began to follow alongside, now, joining their brothers who were mirroring Jason's main army. The flyers continued to lead the way overhead.

Jason marked them all—mechs and flyers alike—as friendlies on his overhead map, and the red dots all turned blue to distinguish them from the green members of his own army.

Only five minutes had passed when one of elliptical flyers plunged out of the sky, trailing a stream of smoke. It crashed into the forest, disintegrating one of the tall pines.

"The Imperials have come," Jhagen said.

J ason watched as the flyers overhead unleashed a barrage of plasma and energy bolts to the north. Many of the vessels were struck by similar bolts in return, and crashed into the ground around Jason's army, sometimes forcing the nearby units to leap out of the way. Jason himself had to dodge as one of those flyers came down in a hail of flames.

Jason tracked the skies above the treetops, but so far he couldn't see any of the attackers that were showing up as red on his overhead map. That would be thanks to his Explorer: he switched to its viewpoint, and picked out white ellipses similar to those of the Modlenth faction, hovering in the distance. A quick count told him that there were over five hundred in view. Potentially more, given that the units could have been concealing others behind them. Meanwhile, there were only two hundred of the flyers with the Modlenth.

"Outnumbered, as usual," Jason said.

"The story of our lives," Tara said.

"That's the way we like it!" Lori said.

"This Lori is my kind of girl," Bokerov commented.

"Eww," Lori said.

Jason sensed movement to the north, between the trees.

There, past the Modlenth mechs, more mechs had emerged. These ones were a dark red in color. Taller than the Modlenth, but not as tall as the War Forgers. They were firing lightning bolts from turrets in their forearms; the Modlenth assumed defensive positions and returned fire with the weapon turrets that had emerged from their own arms. Lightning, plasma, and energy bolts erupted from the lot of them.

Some of the dark red mechs teleported behind the line of Modlenth, and swords unfolded from their forearms, replacing the medium range weapons. They struck out, hewing down the Modlenth mechs from behind.

"I was just about to say, how come none of these mechs seem to have teleport technology?" Tara said.

"Don't just stand there," Jason said. "Help them!" He opened fire with his energy cannon, and struck one of the Teleporters in the back. It fell.

Another red mech teleported behind him. He knew immediately because of the feed from his rear view camera, which he kept piped into the top of his HUD.

Jason switched to Bullet Time, and stepped forward while spinning his body at the same time, and narrowly avoided the sword that the Teleporter attempted to stab through him. He brought his energy weapon to bear, and fired it at point blank range, disintegrating some of the upper body. Fragments erupted from the blast, and shrapnel embedded in his chest area.

"I think they can only teleport once," Tara said. "With at least a minute before they recharge."

She sliced through a Teleporter that appeared behind Aria.

Lori had become invisible, and was unleashing plasma bolts.

Aria fired her lightning bolt weapon at those Teleporters still engaged with the Modlenth. Sophie likewise launched her micro machines at them.

Xin unleashed her plasma beam at an enemy flyer that had closed overhead.

A Teleporter appeared over Iris, and she swiveled her body out of the way of its strike, and caught the mech. She pulled it to the localized energy beam that formed a line between the pincers of her maw, and cut off its head.

"Off with their heads!" Iris cackled.

Maeran's drones swerved in front of Jason, forming a triangular shield as a lightning bolt struck. The shield deflected the blow, hitting a pine tree nearby, and toppling it.

Shaggy and Runt leaped into the fray but before they could latch onto the enemy mechs the units teleported away.

The dogs looked about in confusion.

The enemy mechs dropped down from above, intending to impale both mutants.

But Bruiser and Lackey leaped over their companions, and ripped the dropping mechs out of the air.

Shells arced over the battle, and into the forest where the mechs were emerging. Some were part of Aria's platoon, others belonged to Bokerov.

The Cataphracts, which were near the back of the group, were unleashing their long range weapons at the flyers in the distance, some of which returned fire in kind. It only took a few seconds before all of the enemy flyers turned their attention on the Cataphracts, forcing Bokerov's units to duck beneath the cover of the trees; the enemy flyers promptly concentrated on the Modlenth craft once more.

"There are too many of them!" Jhagan transmitted. "Our only hope is to reach the cover of the Brome!"

"The what?" Sophie said.

"He said Brome!" Lori told her. "An oat like grass sometimes grown for fodder, or ornamental purposes."

"Uh, thanks for the literal definition," Sophie said.

"Quickly, follow the breakaway units!" Jhagan said.

Jason glanced at his overhead map, and saw a series of blue friendlies continuing east away from the battle. Most of the units stayed behind, however, digging in to defend the escapees.

"You heard the alien!" Jason said. "Continue east! Let their mechs fight for us!"

Jason turned away from the incoming Teleporters, and continued east. He sent the Explorer forward to scout the way.

Tara herded the dogs and followed him, along with

the rest of the War Forgers and their clones. The tanks came after them, along with the Cataphracts.

Occasionally, one of the mechs teleported into the trees in front of the War Forgers and managed to get off a strike, either via sword, or the lightning bolt weapon, but the team always mowed down the lone attacker shortly thereafter.

After about two minutes, the Teleporter attacks began to increase as those Modlenth that had remained behind succumbed.

The remaining Modlenth mechs that were escorting Jason's army began to break away in groups to deal with the persistent mech assaults, until only a few escorts were left.

Overhead, the Modlenth flyers were assaulted by an ever-increasing number of bolts; they fell from the sky, at least one every few seconds, crashing into the forest of pines.

Soon some of the enemy flyers were swooping past overhead to launch attacks against the War Forgers. The Arias used their ballistic shields to deflect those blows when they could, while the Sophies fired their jumpjets to similarly intercept the bolts, putting their energy shields to strategic use. Maeran did what she could with her three drones as well.

The others meanwhile remained on the offensive, firing up into those flyers as they passed, and sometimes scoring hits that took them down. Cheyanne also darted up and down, skewering different flyers that got too close to her.

Meanwhile the Teleporters continued to ramp up their ground attacks. Most of them had lost any ability to teleport some time ago, and they relied on rushes now. They were concentrating on the lagging tanks, and some of the War Forgers diverted their attention to the rear to help out.

The Cataphracts were also attacked by some of those Teleporters, but for them, the biggest threats were the flyers, which continued to assail the units. The Sphinx fell under the attacks, and Bokerov was forced to abandon it. The others formed up in single file behind the Axeman, who held his big shield in front of him and deflected most of the blows. That shield was glowing white hot in several places, however, and it was debatable how long it would hold up. That said, the Cataphracts weren't simply on the defensive: they leaned out past the shield to fire their powerful weapons, and usually took down swaths of two to four enemy flyers at once.

"These Imperials are certainly persistent bitches," Tara said.

"Much like yourself," Sophie commented.

"I'll take that as a compliment," Tara said.

Aria 5's shield failed at one point, and she took a blow to the chest, forcing Xin 5 and Sophie 5 to drag her.

Tara 6 also took a devastating blow that took out her power supply, turning her offline. Lori 6 and Julian carried her.

Jason took a blow to the shoulder when a flyer swooped over the treetops and got in a lucky shot. His entire shoulder servomotor disintegrated, and he couldn't move his left arm.

"We're almost there," Jhagan said. "It's less than two kilometers now."

Unfortunately, shortly after Jhagan said those words, a herd of Dragon Cheetahs chose to stage an ambush.

The big creatures plowed through the undergrowth, tearing into the War Forgers from the right.

"Shit!" Jerry said. "Some help here, guys!"

Jason swerved to the right as the enemy flyers continued to swoop down in their overhead attack. Jason fired his energy weapon at a Dragon Cheetah that had Lori 5 pinned, and freed her.

"Thanks, Babe!" Lori 5 said. "I mean, clone of my babe! I mean, original clone. I mean, ah, forget it!"

Tara and Cheyanne were at his side, swords swinging, as Aria drove a wedge into the Dragon Cheetahs with her ballistic shield.

Sophie arced down from above, ripping her micro machines into a Dragon Cheetah that attempted to attack from the side. Runt and Shaggy leaped onto two other bioweapons and began to rip and tear. Bruiser and Lackey did likewise.

The enemy flyers shifted southward, following the War Forgers and their clones. Some of the Dragon Cheetahs leaped skyward and ripped the swooping flyers from the air—they didn't distinguish between the two opposing units. Other flyers, those that remained of the Modlenth, turned back to aid in the defense when they realized that the team had momentarily halted.

Aria had her tanks pummel the bioweapons with

shells and plasma bolts. Bokerov's tanks did likewise as they came within range.

The Cataphracts swerved south, cutting the Dragon Cheetah herd in half, and trampling the big bioweapons underfoot as well as frying them with their weapons.

The Teleporters rushed in from the north, using the opportunity to force Jason and his War Forgers to fight a battle on two fronts. A battle they would quickly lose.

"Push through the Dragon Cheetahs!" Jason said. "Try not to kill them! Let them slow down the Teleporters!"

With the Arias and their ballistic shields in the lead, Jason and the others shoved their way forward. Jason fired his energy weapon when he was able—he had to wait a minute between each shot to recharge enough to fire again. The others were similarly restricted, except those with swords—the Taras, and Cheyanne. They used their weapons sparingly, trying to cause injury, rather than to kill, and mostly to deter the Dragon Cheetahs from attacking. Sometimes those bioweapons breathed those super-heated slugs at them, but either Aria absorbed the blast with her shield, or Jason and the others ducked or sidestepped.

They reached the Cataphracts, and then swerved east. Bokerov's tanks followed behind them.

Some of the Dragon Cheetahs pursued, hounding the rear ranks where the Cataphracts resided, but most turned to the seemingly easier foe—the Teleporters.

The plan was working.

As Jason and the others continued eastward, they had only the flyers overhead to deal with. Cheyanne darted occasionally to cut down a flyer as it swooped past; the others mostly defended, as they waiting for the sun to recharge their batteries enough to continue firing.

The trees abruptly ended, opening into an exposed plain. Ahead of the War Forgers, about eight hundred meters distance, was a shimmering, golden dome. It was translucent, and Jason could see the hint of buildings beyond. He didn't pay those structures much attention, because he was focused on the flyers that continued to assail from overhead.

He realized that the enemy flyers were zig-zagging, while the Modlenth flyers had formed a sturdy line up ahead. At the base of the dome there was a silver ring, seemingly the source of the energy field. From that ring many turrets protruded, and they were launching bolts of energy, lightning, and electricity at the enemy fliers. There were also a few laser turrets among them, though of course Jason couldn't see the beams they produced, as the photons were not of the visible spectrum.

"The Brome," Jhagan said.

"I think he means dome," Lori said.

Jason hurried forward across the plains, toward that dome. There was an arched entrance within the silver ring at the base of the dome; several Modlenth mechs waited there. They stood in dual lines, one on either side of the entrance.

The attacks continued, but dwindled the closer the team got to the dome.

Aria led the way past those ranks of Modlenth, and toward the arched opening. Beyond was a rectangular passage.

She hurried inside, and Jason followed. The passage was just tall enough to fit his mech, with a width that could hold three of them abreast. In moments the entirety of the War Forgers had entered, and the team formed three columns. The Rex Wolves also fit, and resided just behind Jason and the main group.

"There isn't room for your entire army," Jhagan said. "Especially the larger robot variants at your rear. But we will ensure their safety while they remain outside."

Jason turned around to regard the plains beyond the opening. The attacks had essentially ceased, with Bokerov's tanks only occasionally launching a shell into the air and the Cataphracts not firing at all. Meanwhile, the defense turrets continued pounding the fleeing enemy forces.

"Bokerov, you'll have to wait outside," Jason said.

"Ah, as usual," Bokerov said. "I do the brunt of the work, and I'm not even invited into the house for dinner."

The tanks came to a halt near the line of Modlenth mechs outside, and as Jason watched, the entrance irised closed, sealing the War Forgers and their clones within the compartment.

9

J ason kept an eye on his overhead map, and confirmed that Bokerov and his troops weren't under attack—their data signals were able to pass through the sealed gate. At least for now.

Jason was near the forefront of the column of War Forgers and their clones; he turned around until he was facing a ramp that led to a pair of big, metal double doors beside him. The roof sloped upward to match that ramp, so he wouldn't have to duck when he climbed the latter.

Beside the doors, there was a smaller alcove, which opened now, revealing another Modlenth mech. Like the others, it was half the size of Jason's mech, and humanoid in shape, excepting the four grasping arms.

It spoke with the voice of Jhagan over the comm band.

"Only a few of you may stand in the presence of the

Central," Jhagan said. "Please select no more than nine members."

"What about the dogs?" Tara said.

Jhagan glanced at the Rex Wolves, which were growling at him. "Even if they were allowed, they wouldn't be able to breathe the air."

"I don't suppose I can have my Explorer lead the way?" Jason nodded toward the scout that hovered in front of him.

"No," Jhagan said. "Unauthorized flyers will be shot down."

"Too bad." Jason recalled the Explorer and docked it in his storage compartment. "All right, War Forgers. All Originals, with me. Cheyanne, Iris, and Maeran, you come, too. Clones, stay here. If you don't hear from us in two hours, cut your way forcibly out of here, and take the army as far away as you can. John, you'll be in charge if we don't return."

"You'll be back," John insisted.

"Thanks for the vote of confidence," Jason said. "But if not, you're in charge, got it?"

"I do," John said.

"Good. You might as well activate your repair drones in the meantime." Jason activated his own, and the drones began repairing the damage he'd taken outside. He stepped toward Jhagan.

"You will have to turn those off in the presence of the Central," Jhagan said. "Repairs are considered rude. And although they hover close to your mechs, they might be considered unauthorized flyers, and shot down."

"Tell me when we're almost there," Jason said. At first, he wondered how Jhagan even knew what they were, but he realized Bokerov had probably shared a few mech designs with these aliens, including the location and blueprints of their repair drones.

The Modlenth mech walked up the ramp, toward the pair of double doors. When Jhagan reached them, the doors parted, and he passed through into the golden light beyond.

Jason assumed it was an airlock of some kind, because of the comment Jhagan had made about the Rex Wolves not being able to breathe the air beyond. He glanced at Lori and Tara on either side of him, then over his shoulder at the others. "Well, I guess it's time. Taras 2 and 3, restrain the dogs, if you will."

The respective Taras came forward and grabbed onto the Rex Wolves by their napes, and spoke soothing words to the animals.

Meanwhile, Jason passed through the opening, and realized it wasn't an airlock after all—he had entered the city proper. And the atmospheric content had already changed: the air was clearer here, not tinged with yellow mist. Looking back, he saw some sort of atmospheric membrane lining the doorway—obviously the Tyrnari equivalent of an airlock, meant to keep the outer gases at bay.

"The atmosphere has changed," Aria confirmed when she entered behind him.

Jason continued forward, giving room for the other core members of his War Forgers to step through.

Meanwhile, he examined his surroundings with

great interest. He traveled on what could best be described as a city street. Lining it on either side were tall, triangular buildings. Their gold surfaces had lines of bright yellow light cutting across them horizontally at intervals—windows, Jason guessed. Those in the current section were about the same height as he was. Visibility was quite high, thanks to the lack of yellow mist in the atmosphere, and he could see all the way to the city center several blocks away, where the buildings were much higher, reaching toward the distant top of the energy dome that enveloped the entire city. The taller buildings clustered at different heights around one central building, which towered above them all.

The golden glow emitted by all of those buildings suffused the city, casting everything in a gentle yellow light. It was warmer than the mist of the atmosphere outside.

Overhead, egg shaped flyers moved to and fro in designated skylanes. It was similar to the air traffic that could be found in an Earth metropolis, actually.

The ground seemed to be made of some translucent material layered over a gold substrate; it couldn't have been pure glass, because it was strong enough to hold the weight of the mechs without cracking. The surface also seemed slightly slippery, and Jason was careful to plant his feet firmly with each step.

He heard a gentle thud behind him; glancing at his rear view video feed, he realized the double doors had sealed behind Cheyanne, Iris, and Maeran, the last of the War Forgers to step through. Lori, Tara, Sophie, Aria and Xin were also present, as requested.

Jhagan continued forward, and Jason increased his pace so that he was walking at the mech's side. It was almost like walking beside a child, or dwarf, in Jason's eyes.

On a side street, he saw smaller, tentacled creatures sliding across the translucent surface of the roadway. If Jhagan's mech was a child, these beings were babies compared to the War Forgers.

The main bodies were vaguely jellyfish-like—thin, bluish sacs that dimpled slightly as they moved, seemingly inflated by some sort of liquid within. The sacs were slightly translucent, allowing Jason to observe the street beyond, but otherwise he couldn't see any sign of internal organs.

Tentacled appendages hung down to several starfish-like feet that were spread wide across the glassy ground; as the creatures advanced, those extremities moved in a sweeping motion that never left the surface. The slippery nature of the material coating the ground was likely purposeful, and probably aided the locomotion of the creatures. Then again, Jason noticed thin trails of slime were left in the wake of those feet. Could the slippery quality of the surface be due to that? No, wait... the trails seemed to evaporate from the roadway after a few moments.

"Tyrnari?" Jason asked.

"Good guess," Jhagan replied.

"So this is how they look outside their mechs," Tara said. "That would explain why they need to live inside domes."

"We captured one before, if you'll recall, inside a

Phaser mech" Aria said. "When I dissected it, I found nothing inside. No internal organs. No muscle fibers. No brain."

"True," Tara said. "This is the first time we've seen living Tyrnari. What did we conclude about their lack of organs?"

"Jason suggested they stored their organs in some higher dimension," Xin said.

"That's right," Aria said. "Well, they must store them somewhere, if they're sentient enough to communicate with us. Hey Jason, ask them where they keep their internal organs."

"You do it," Jason said.

"Er, Alien, where do you keep your internal organs?" Aria said.

"It's best if we don't reveal too much, at this point," Jhagan said.

"That's hardly fair, given what you know about humanity," Tara said.

"We have the advantage, I admit," Jhagan said. "But that is due to the forthcoming nature of your comrade, Bokerov. Blame him for the unfairness of your current situation."

Jhagan continued down the main pathway toward the downtown core, which was free of the Tyrnari pedestrians who dominated the side streets. Even so, Jason kept an eye on where he stepped: it wouldn't do to accidentally squish one of their hosts. That might piss off this Central of theirs.

"We just lost contact with the clones, and the rest of the army," Aria said. "We're on our own."

So far, none of their repair drones had been shot down for being "unauthorized flyers." Because of that, Jason considered launching his Explorer to get a bird's eye view of the city, but decided that would be pushing it.

Soon the triangular buildings increased in height, beginning to reach into the sky. Gazing up, some almost seemed to brush the energy dome just over-head. Because of the concave nature of that dome, the height was lower here, than in the exact center of the city.

"So, Risilan, this Central, is your leader?" Jason said.

"Correct," Jhagan said.

"Tell me about him," Jason said.

"*Her*," Jhagan corrected.

"Her, then," Jason said.

"She would be a considered a princess among your kind," Jhagan said. "We adore her."

"Whoa, we're going to meet a real life princess!" Lori said. "I'm so excited!"

"I bet you're jealous, Sophie," Tara said. "Seeing as how you're a princess wannabe."

"Not at all," Sophie said. "Why would I be jealous? This 'princess' is an alien. She has a slimy body, tenta-cles for arms, starfish for feet. No competition whatso-ever for me."

"Teehee!" Lori said. "You've seen what *you* look like right? A human torso plastered onto a spider's body? You'd certainly give the aliens a run for the money in the ugly department!"

"Uh, my external form doesn't count," Sophie said. "My avatar is the real me."

"Maybe this Princess Risilan has an avatar form, too," Tara said. "Compatible with our VR systems."

"Oh, shit," Sophie said. "I hadn't thought of that. Then again, I can't see why Jason would be interested in a creature like that. I mean come on, look at them. They're all slimy and gross."

"VR can mask a lot of imperfections…" Tara said.

"You wouldn't be interested in an alien woman, right Jason?" Sophie said.

"That's right," Jason replied. He hadn't been listening that intently. He was concentrating on the alien buildings around him, and wondering what this Central wanted from him.

"There, see?" Sophie said. "We have nothing to worry about."

"Jhagan, can I get a hint at what Risilan wants?" Jason said.

"Sorry," Jhagan said. "She will explain it in person, as I told you before."

The group had reached the city center and were completely surrounded by those huge triangular skyscrapers. Jhagan continued toward the central building that towered over them all.

"It kind of makes sense that the Central would reside here," Tara said as she gazed at that big building.

Jhagan glanced at her mech, and followed her gaze to the main skyscraper.

"Actually, she does not," Jhagan said. He diverted toward a smaller building nestled between two skyscrapers. It was still huge, however, easily fitting at least a hundred War Forger mechs inside. This one differed from the others in that it was pyramidal in shape, rather than triangular. It was surrounded by a wall with triangular towers placed at each of its four corners—well, Jason couldn't see the farther two corners because of the size of that pyramid, but he assumed more towers were located there. He could see small triangular outlines near the tops of those towers; he guessed they were hidden panels that contained weapon turrets.

Jhagan approached the wall. It was about the same height as the alien mech, or roughly half the size of Jason's.

"This is where the Central lives," Jhagan said.

A gap materialized in the wall, giving enough room for each of the mechs to enter in turn.

They did so.

Jhagan approached the towering pyramid, and a similar gap materialized, revealing a triangular corridor that could fit three War Forgers at once.

Jhagan paused. "Please deactivate your repair drones."

Jason and the others recalled their repair units, and the drones flew into their associated storage compartments.

"Those are not allowed, either," Jhagan said, nodding toward the three drones that orbited Maeran.

Maegan issued an instruction, and the three drones promptly landed on her shoulder regions. "Good?"

"Yes," Jhagan said.

Jhagan entered, and Jason followed with Tara and Lori at his side.

"Why does it feel like we're stepping past the point of no return?" Tara asked.

"Probably because we are," Jason said. "Whatever happens in here, will define our futures forever."

"Not just ours," Lori said. "Humanity's."

10

J ason stood in a central chamber in the heart of the pyramid. Four walls, sloping at the same angle as the exterior surfaces, met at the apex far above. Thick support pillars held up those sloping walls. Standing between these pillars were other four-armed mechs like the one Jhagan operated. Their weapon turrets were on full display on the forearm sections. Currently, those weapons were pointed at the ground.

The pillars formed a path from the entrance to the far side of the big chamber, where a small dais held a lone Tyrnari, apparently seated, judging from the way those tentacles were folded underneath the body. On the floor next to the dais resided other Tyrnari, these ones standing. Several more of the aliens lined the wall behind the dais; they had metallic cylinders affixed to the midpoints of their appendages. Probably weapons.

The alien seated upon the dais was nearly identical to the others in terms of jellyfish-like shape, and those tentacles with the starfish feet. But Jason did notice an extra appendage behind the sac of its body, almost a topknot of sorts because of its bristly, hair like nature. He couldn't tell if the topknot was some form of clothing, or a natural part of the alien.

There was also the obvious blur of an active energy field in front of that particular Tyrnari. A spherical protective enclosure of some kind. A good precaution, he supposed.

There was enough room in the chamber for Jason and the others to cross to that dais, but Jhagan had waved for the team to stop as soon as all of them had stepped inside. Another good precaution.

Jhagan had the War Forgers spread out along the wall behind them. Jason remained near the center, staring down between the pillars toward the dais, and the alien it contained.

"Greetings," a woman's voice came over the comm. "I am Risilan."

"See, no avatar!" Sophie said triumphantly.

"Sh!" Jason said. "It's good to finally meet you, Princess."

"Call me Central," Risilan said. "Princess is a human term."

"My apologies," Jason said. He waited for her to say more, but when she wasn't forthcoming, he added: "So. You wanted to see us."

Still no response.

He decided to wait. He realized she was likely judging his every action, gauging his responses, trying to determine his character, and intent. He was doing the same, of course. And he refused to cave first.

Finally Risilan spoke once more. "I am the rightful queen of all Tyrnari."

Jason was somewhat stunned by the news. Rather than voicing his surprise, he decided to wait for her to say more.

"The current royal family killed my father, the rightful king of the Tyrnari," Risilan continued. "They slew most of my brothers and sisters, but the new king took pity on me, and instead tried to send me into exile on a colony world. My most loyal guards freed me, and I escaped here to this city, where my most loyal followers resided."

"So wait a second, this isn't a staging planet?" Jason said. "Meant to launch attacks against my homeworld?"

"No," Risilan said. "This is the Tyrnari homeworld itself."

"But the air…" Jason said. "I transported bioweapons from Earth here, with my army. They were able to breathe the atmosphere outside this energy dome, and were part of the bioweapons the original invaders sent to Earth. The Banthar. What are the chances of that?"

"Unfortunately, we turned this world into a bioweapon breeding ground many centuries ago, to please the empire," Risilan said. "So of course these bioweapons of yours can breathe here if they were sent by the Banthar, who are also empire members."

"You terraformed your entire planet to please an empire?" Jason said.

"They are a powerful empire," Risilan said. "Turning them down wouldn't have been a wise move. We had to clear the plains of natural life, move to the cities, and envelop them all in protective domes. In exchange, we had the favor of the empire. The prime space lanes. Authorization to build a complete space navy. Plus, the production of bioweapons for the empire provided a much needed boost to our staggering world economy, and attracted several new trade outposts, as well as investments from other member species of the empire."

"That's what you told the common people when you sold them on the deal, I bet," Jason said. "And sure, it sounds great on digital paper, until you realize you've ruined your world in the process."

"Yes," Risilan said. "And unfortunately, because my family was involved in the decision, it ignited the spark that eventually led to our downfall."

"This is the future Bokerov would have forced upon humanity," Jason commented on a private line. "By allowing our planet to be terraformed, and driving us into domes merely to survive."

"A future we haven't avoided yet," Tara said.

Jason switched to the band the alien was using. "Why are you telling me all of this?"

"I have a proposition to make," Risilan replied.

"I'm listening," Jason said.

"I want you to help me sack the Imperial city," Risilan said.

"Uh, I'm guessing this is a big city," Jason said. "It's well defended. With a substantial army."

"Good guess," Risilan said.

"Why would you need our help?" Jason said. "I'm sure you have technology vastly superior to our own?"

"Some," Risilan said. "But we've seen some of the weaponry you humans have stolen from the Banthar. Some of those weapons we ourselves don't have."

"Yeah, we didn't exactly reverse engineer the tech," Jason said. "You see, the Banthar were a little careless. They employed neural interfaces with some of their weapons, embedding them in organics. To use the weapons, all we had to do was cut out part of the brain stems, and stimulate them with our own primitive technology."

"Spies tell me you employed energy weapons stolen from the Tyrnari as well," Risilan said. "At least, your specific group. Your War Forgers, as you call them."

"Oh yeah," Jason said. "Those. Yes. Again, the interface was mostly already there, and just required a few electrical impulses to get going. I'm guessing the empire supplied you with these weapons, and you don't really know how they work yourselves."

"Some of them are black boxes to us, yes," Risilan said. "With a standard interface that can be linked to a bioweapon."

"There you go," Jason said. "So you didn't exactly answer my question. Unless you're trying to tell me that you want us to fight for you because we have some weapons we borrowed from the Banthar."

"No," Risilan said. "Mostly, I request your assistance because of the size of your army."

"It isn't exactly all that large," Jason said. "I'm sure you have a bigger army protecting this city itself."

"Actually, we don't," Risilan said. "My army has slowly been ravaged over the years. The defenses you saw outside the dome hold up well when the Imperials send a few skirmishers, as they did with you, but—"

"That was more than a few," Jason interrupted.

"Yes, but when they dispatch their actual army, that's when the trouble comes. Fortunately for us, they've sent most of their army to your planet at the moment," Risilan said.

"Wait, you're trying to tell me the Imperials don't have another army here to protect themselves?" Jason said. "That they've left themselves open to attack? Why would they do that? Unless they were idiots…"

"Not idiots," Risilan said. "The Empire has strict quotas on how big of a local army each member system is allowed. Colonies are even more restricted. We've negotiated a bigger space navy than normal, thanks to our willingness to terraform our planet for the empire, but local troop numbers are restricted. The Imperials are compelled to obey the quotas. Since we're not officially associated with the empire, we don't necessarily have to obey that particular edict."

"But you're part of the same planet," Jason said. "I doubt this empire would recognize multiple factions. What if they found out what you are doing? Wouldn't they attack?"

"They'd certainly quell our numbers, and the Imperials would lose power in the process," Risilan said. "Which is why the Imperials would never tell them. And also why they stage routine attacks to keep our troop numbers in check."

"What about all these bioweapons you claim are produced here?" Jason said. "Why wouldn't the Imperials just gather them all up and use them to defend their city if they needed to?"

"Using the bioweapons for anything other than officially designated empire purposes, such as local skirmishes, is strictly prohibited, and punishable by death to the involved parties," Risilan said.

"This empire doesn't sound like a very friendly organization," Jason said.

"Try to avoid joining, if you can," Risilan said. "Perhaps you will get lucky. Perhaps they will overlook your technology, considering it a backwater world, and you will surprise them, developing weapons technology surpassing their own, so that when you finally attract their attention, you will be ready. But most likely, not."

"So these bioweapons are allowed to roam the plains, attacking whatever they want, until the Imperials capture them?" Jason asked.

"That's right," Risilan said. "The bulls are rounded up, packaged, and shipped out in quarterly culls."

"Nice," Jason said. "So since using the bioweapons is prohibited... these Imperials have committed most of their army to Earth, leaving them open to an attack here..."

"Correct," Risilan said. "But their numbers are still formidable, at least without you to help me, given the current state of my army. Also, now that the main Imperial army is on Earth, they have no limits to the number of units they can produce, since your home-world is outside empire rule. Which is why they took the Creation Structures with them, and will run them at all hours to produce more troops, especially if there are raw materials available. In a few days, they will very likely send back these newly produced reinforcements. Our window of opportunity is short."

"So do you have a specific plan?" Jason asked.

"You will be part of the initial strike force," Risilan said.

"So cannon fodder, basically…" Jason said.

"Not at all," Risilan said. "Assuming I'm under-standing the idiom correctly. Our own troops will also be among you. You will attack the city from the west. The Imperials will commit roughly half of their troops to stave off the attack. When they do, a second Modlenth strike force will attack from the east. The Imperials will send the remainder of their forces to engage them. Meanwhile, while the two of you keep the defenders occupied, a smaller, third group, led by myself, will make a headlong rush into the city from the north, directly to the Imperial palace. I will kill the royal family and all the heirs, assume my rightful place, and then call off the forces attacking you."

"Sounds bloody," Jason said.

"Uprisings usually are," Risilan said.

"You're sure you have a way to defeat the defenses of the Imperial palace once you're in the city?" Jason pressed. "I doubt they'll be light."

"I have friends in the Imperial palace," Risilan said.

"They will help me when my precision strike force is in place."

"Does the success of the operation depend on these 'friends' of yours?" Jason said.

"No," Risilan said. "If they don't help, we'll break through the defenses ourselves. It will simply take longer."

"I'm not sure I like the part about killing the royal family and all the heirs," Jason said.

"Neither do I!" Lori said on a private channel.

"Maybe you can kill the emperor alone," Jason said. "And leave the heirs alone?"

"Unacceptable," Risilan said. "There must be no one left alive who could ever attempt to resume power. If I spared anyone of royal blood, I would merely be planting the seeds for the next coup. That would be irresponsible, not to mention immoral, for all of the citizenry who would die in the coming wars."

Jason didn't know what to say.

"So you will not help, given these conditions?" Risilan said.

"Depends," Jason said. "What do we get in return?"

"What do you want?" Risilan said.

"Will you promise to return us to Earth?" Jason asked.

"I can certainly do that, once we are successful," Risilan said. "Because I will have control of the rift generators."

"How about lending me some of your army as well," Jason said. "So I can defeat the Tyrnari waiting on the other side? I don't really want them to terraform our planet…"

"We won't need to lend you any troops," Risilan said. "If we're successful, the Imperials will recall their entire army, returning them here in an attempt to deal with me. Your homeworld will be free of their influence."

"Aren't you worried that they'll have more troops than they left with?" Jason said. "Thanks to those, what did you call them… Creation Structures?"

"This is true," Risilan said. "At least, assuming the native defense forces of your planet fail to make any difference in their numbers. But I'll have control of our space navy by then. I'll recall the warships, and they will help me destroy the army with attacks from orbit."

"I won't be staying around for that," Jason said.

"It's not one of the requirements," Risilan said. "I only need your army for the initial strike against the Imperial city."

"Good," Jason said. "Then I think we have a deal. When do we leave?"

"I will gather my army," Risilan said. "And join you outside the dome in two hours."

11

J ason and his War Forgers followed Jhagan's mech out of the city.

"How far is it to the Imperial city?" Jason asked the alien along the way.

"Not long," Jhagan said. "A day's march, if that. We can only move as fast as our slowest units, of course. And that would be you. Or more specifically, those vehicles you call tanks."

"Yeah, nothing we can do about that," Jason said.

"Some upgrades might be in order at a future date," Jhagan said. "But for now, yes, there is nothing you can do."

When Jason was back in comm range with the rest of the army, he informed them of the new agreement.

"Well, I don't really care how we get home," Tara 5 said. "Even if we have to destroy a royal family to do it."

"I hope I get to kill some alien royals!" Bokerov said.

"Actually, you won't," Jason said. "We're part of the diversionary force."

"Damn it," Bokerov said. "I never get to have any fun. What's the point of obeying you if I can't do what I want once in a while?"

"Because you're compelled to," Jason said.

He reached the exit to the dome, and traveled through the airlock membrane and into the rectangular compartment beyond. The Rex Wolves yipped excitedly when they saw him and the others.

Shaggy leaped on his chest, and licked his face.

"Hey Shag," Jason said. "Nice to see you, too." He glanced at the overhead map and confirmed that Julian and his clones were near the exit on the far side of the compartment. "Julian, lead the way out."

"But the doors—" Julian began.

They irised open as he spoke, and Julian directed his War Forger clones outside. Jason waited for the others to exit, and then he followed with his Originals. He exited, passing between the dual ranks of Modlenth mechs, and took up a position next to the waiting tanks and Cataphracts.

Two hours later, Risilan's army joined them. It was composed of a thousand elliptical ships, five hundred mechs, and a hundred airships. Most of the latter seemed big enough to be cargo ships.

Jason had a direct line to Jhagan, who would be his battle leader during the fight. Jhagan would also relay any orders to him from Risilan.

"Jhagan, what kind of cargo are those airships

carrying?" Jason asked. "Or are they simply troop carriers?"

"Just a few bioweapons our scientists have cooked up," Jhagan replied. "A little something to surprise the Imperials with."

"I'm looking forward to that!" Bokerov said.

"So Risilan is really breaking all the empire's rules," Jason said. "Creating a personal army that puts her entire planet over the limit allowed by the empire. Deploying bioweapons, when the creatures are only allowed to fight for the empire."

"When she assumes control, one day the empire will attack," Jhagan said. "It will be many years from now, however. Perhaps decades."

"Why so long?" Jason asked.

"Haven't you guessed?" Jhagan said. "Why do you think the empire needs bioweapons so badly from its member species? They are engaged in a war. One that has lasted almost two centuries. They don't have the resources to commit to quelling every little uprising that comes along, at least not immediately. They will deal with us when there is a respite in the war."

"I'd hate to meet whatever enemy the empire is fighting," Jason said.

"So would we," Jhagan said.

"Have you ever seen this enemy?" Jason asked.

"Not directly," Jhagan replied.

Jason waited for him to tell him more, but he had a feeling Jhagan wasn't going to be all that forthcoming on the subject.

It's just going to have to be another one of those mysteries of the universe.

As the army set out, Jason scanned the alien ranks, trying to guess where Risilan was cloistered. In the mech regiment, he spotted a Modlenth with a white topknot protruding from the metal head area, one that matched the topknot Risilan herself wore.

He was about to ask Jhagan about it, but decided the alien probably wouldn't tell him. Instead, he went with: "You know, it's interesting how your mech design diverges so drastically from your actual bodies."

"We design for utility, rather than beauty," Jhagan said.

And that was the end of their conversation.

Jason's army followed behind the main group of Modlenth. The War Forgers went first, forming five columns organized by clone, followed by the tanks, with the Cataphracts at the rear. Those Cataphracts reached as high as the airships Risilan possessed.

The terrain was relatively flat for the first hour, then became slightly hilly in the second. A new type of tree began to dominate the surroundings, this one more like a sprawling oak. It had a long, bare trunk that reached well above Jason's mech, with branches at the top expanding outward in an umbrella-like pattern; those branches were covered in the same silky, web-like leaves of the previous pines.

"Furry Umbrellas!" Lori said. "That's what I'm calling them."

"You would," Sophie said.

Soon the army was treading though a forest of those

trees, which heights concealed even the Cataphracts, not to mention the airships.

"This forest will take us right to the city," Jhagan said. "We've sent scouts ahead to hack into the surveillance units the Imperials have scattered throughout the trees. They will replace the camera feeds with video loops, allowing us to approach undetected. At least, that's the plan."

"Thanks for the update," Jason said.

A few minutes later Jhagan told him: "We'll be passing close to a bioweapon breeding facility in a few minutes. Don't be alarmed by what you see. A containment field keeps the bioweapons penned in."

Sure enough, after five minutes, the trees to the right fell away. Jason saw a group of Dragon Cheetahs inside an energy dome, separated from a herd of Girahips in another. There was also another kind of bioweapon he'd never seen before in a different dome: basically it looked like a bunch of elephant trunks attached to a crab-like body. Those trunks moved randomly, feeling out the air above them; when they actually brushed against the swaying trunk of a nearby bioweapon, both trunks tightened, and pulled toward each other, so that the two entities soon became intertwined, with all of their trunks gripping their twins. One of the two inevitably stood on the ground, while the other had its six legs crimped skyward. And then, after a few moments, the trunks would slowly release when the bioweapons realized they were contacting a friendly, and the trunks unzipped, and they were back on their feet, trunks swaying in the air once more.

It was all rather disgusting, really.

Jason's gaze was drawn to the Dragon Cheetah pen: those particular bioweapons were leaping toward the passing mechs en masse, but were inevitably stopped by the containment field, which flashed brighter where contact was made. It didn't matter that hundreds of troops had passed by before Jason and the others: the Dragon Cheetahs just kept relentlessly throwing themselves at the field, like they couldn't help themselves.

"Obviously they're programmed to strike at anything that moves," Tara said.

"Which explains why they were so eager to divert from their regular prey back in the pine forest," Aria said. "When we passed a few that were on the loose."

"That was more than a few," Sophie said.

"You think the Modlenth replaced any camera feeds inside there?" Lori asked.

"They must have," Xin replied. "Otherwise the Imperials would be dispatching a team to find out what was exciting their bioweapons."

"Why do I think those crabs with the elephant trunks are cute?" Cheyanne said.

"Because you're one sick individual," Maeran said.

"Thank you," Cheyanne said. "Coming from you, that means a lot to me."

"You know, for as long as I've known you two girls, I still don't get your humor," Aria said.

"You will, someday," Cheyanne said. "It's an acquired taste."

The forest soon replaced the facility, and Jason continued the march without having to worry that those

Dragon Cheetahs might break free. Actually, that wasn't entirely true. He kept glancing at his rear view feed for the next ten minutes until he was certain none of those bioweapons had broken loose to pursue.

That didn't mean other bioweapons might not attack somewhere along the way, of course.

"Hey Jhagan," Jason said. "What are the chances we might be attacked by bioweapons en route? I mean, considering we had two encounters with these Dragon Cheetahs of yours so far. It seems like there are a lot of the things on the loose."

"Low, I'd say," Jhagan said. "The first time you were unlucky. The second time, well, the battle drew them. That, and your larger units, which had their upper bodies poking out of the forest, visible for kilometers around. Here, that can't happen."

"But what about our noise?" Jason said. "And the vibrations we produce?"

"Those are masked as well," Jhagan said. "Part of the stealth tech we Tyrnari have produced. In addition to the video loops, the stealth tech will mask our approach to the city, until it's too late."

"Oh," Jason said. "I wonder how that works."

Jhagan didn't answer.

"Don't want to reveal your tech, huh?" Jason said. Still no answer. "By the way, how come there are so many bioweapons out there anyway? You'd think the Imperials would spend time hunting them down. Lost profits and all, right?"

"You can blame the Modlenth for that," Jhagan said. "We sometimes attack their breeding facilities and purposely set their bioweapons free. At first the Imperials rounded them up as fast as they were able, like you said, but eventually we wore them down, and they gave up. They've since shored up the defenses of their facilities, and we don't attack them nearly as often as we did in the past. These days, the Imperials only round up escaped bioweapons when they need to meet empire quotas."

"Can the creatures breed out there?" Jason said. "Outside the facilities?"

"Of course," Jhagan said. "Which is why we didn't really put that great of a dent in overall bioweapon production. Sometimes we stage hunting parties to eradicate as many freed bioweapons as we can, but inevitably there are a few we miss, and their populations bounce back."

"Interesting."

About three hours into the march Jason received a VR request. Wondering which of the girls was bothering him now, he was surprised when he read the name next to the request: Risilan.

So Bokerov shared his VR code with the Tyrnari as well. Interesting.

"Z, take control of my mech," Jason said. "I'll be entering VR for a little while."

"Affirmative," Z said. "It looks like the alien princess wants to play with you."

"Yeah, well, I guess we'll just have to see what she wants," Jason said.

"Don't do anything I wouldn't do," Z told him with a seductive rasp to her voice.

"Uh, yeah," Jason said.

He switched his consciousness to his loading screen and created a new VR partition for privacy, seeing as all the girls had access to his main VR. Then he loaded up a copy of his mountain lake house.

He walked out to the picnic table and sat down on the main table portion.

He rubbed his chin. "Hmm. Not here."

He teleported to the family room of his house. He sat down on the hardwood floor next to a floor-to-ceiling window overlooking the lake.

Then he accepted the VR request.

A woman appeared in front of him.

Her face was pale, with long, curly red hair that reached below the front of her shoulders. Her cheeks were rouged, her eyelids painted in dark blue eye shadow for a smoky effect. A tear-drop brooch hung down from the center of her head, from a small tiara she wore just above her hairline.

A see-through yellow veil was draped over her locks a few centimeters past the hairline, a veil that reached all the way to her waist. She wore two pearl necklaces placed one atop the other; they were tight, neatly wrapping her neck, the first made of silver pearls, the second black. She also had on two groups of longer necklaces. The first group was made of closely spaced red beads that reached below her breasts. The second group of necklaces was slightly longer, reaching to her navel, and covered in bigger, golden beads that were more widely dispersed.

Her gown was red and gold, with white sleeves, and

so long that it hid her feet. She had a tall brown belt cinching the garment at the middle, and she wore golden bracelets on her wrists, and rings on her fingers.

She looked very much how he would have imagined a princess.

Jason cocked an eyebrow. "Risilan?"

She smiled. "Hello."

"You've been researching Earth princesses, I see," Jason said.

The smile became a frown. "Is my form not pleasing by human beauty standards?"

"Uh, yeah, sure," Jason said. "But one thing you quickly learn about us humans, everyone is beautiful in VR."

"I see," Risilan said. "Perhaps I should use my Tyrnari form."

"No," Jason said. "This one is much more pleasing on the eyes."

She nodded. "Very well."

"So what did you want?" Jason said.

"Only to acquaint myself with the human I'm trusting to help me secure the throne," Risilan said.

"Well, there's not much you really need to know about me, I think," Jason said. "I'm from Earth. That's good enough, isn't it?"

"Would you rather I left you alone?" Risilan said.

"No," Jason said. "You can stay."

"Good." Risilan sat down on the floor in front of him. She bent her knees, so that her calves partially rested against the insides of her thighs, and the lower part of the gown spread out around her.

She looked really good, he had to admit.

I might have to talk to the other girls about dressing up like this.

"You know, you probably shouldn't be giving away the position of the mech you're using with that topknot," Jason said.

Her brow furrowed, but then she seemed to realize what he was talking about.

"That particular mech is part of my royal guard," Risilan said. "It's a ruse: I'm in an unmarked mech nearby."

"Ah," Jason said. "Good job."

"The Imperials know this already," Risilan said. "They've tried to assassinate me several times since I refused to live in exile."

"It must be hard, being a princess," Jason said. "At least on your world."

"You don't have princesses on yours?" Risilan asked.

"Well, we do," Jason said. "But they have no real power. Sure, they can influence politics to an extent, inasmuch as they can sway their followers, but otherwise, they're just like any other rich people who have to resort to lobbying to get what they want. My homeworld isn't ruled by a single man or woman, or a family. We've divided our planet into different countries, based on territory. Each of these countries run elections, where—"

"Yes, I've read about your political systems," Risilan said. "Ours is much more efficient. You waste time and effort, not to mention your 'credits,' to run elections every two years. There is no such thing as stability:

elected officials are always changing. With us, the same people are always in charge. We ensure peace and prosperity for our people, giving wealth to those who deserve it, and pain to those who do not."

"Sounds like a despot system, to me," Jason said.

"You cannot understand," Risilan said. "You are an alien."

"Yeah, and here I thought you were the alien," Jason said. "But I can see your point of view. I'm the one who's come to *your* homeworld, after all."

"Yes," Risilan said. "Our ruling system fits perfectly with the Tyrnari mindset. Any other system would fail. Believe me. We've even tried some of the systems your species practices. They all ended in bloodshed."

"And yours didn't?" Jason said. "You murder each other in coups every few years. Plus, you allowed your entire planet to be terraformed to produce bioweapons for the empire."

"The terraforming would have happened regardless," Risilan said. "And the coups, they will end once I am back in power."

"So you say," Jason said.

"They will end," she said firmly. She stared plasma bolts into his eyes, but then at last sighed, and sat back. "Coups. Such a detestable thing." She clutched her veil in one hand, and her eyes glazed over. "I still remember the day the Imperials slaughtered my family. Duke Malbeck was visiting under the pretense of tribute negotiations. Among his guard, he hid assassins. When my father welcomed him with open arms, his assassins vomited up hidden weapons, and killed him. They hunted down my family members. I still remember hiding in the kitchens, hearing the screams of my brothers. I couldn't have been more than five years old, in Earth terms."

"I'm sorry," Jason said. He paused. "But you know, it sounds like this is more about vengeance than anything else."

She looked at him. "Vengeance is a part. But I truly want to help my people. I plan to shut down bioweapon production when I'm back in command. I want to restore our homeworld to the way it once was, so that Tyrnari may walk free among the plains once more, rather than living their lives inside the dome cities."

"The empire won't like that, I take it," Jason said.

She shrugged. "We will lose our position in the High Council. And we'll probably have to ax our space navy. But it will be worth it."

"Jhagan told me the empire would one day attack when you became queen," Jason said.

She nodded. "It's possible. They don't like royal dynasties changing hands without their approval. I'm hoping I'll be able to negotiate my way out of any attack. But if they decide to make an example out of me, then we will fight. We'll use our space navy against them, rather than giving it up."

"So wait, if what you said is true, that means these Imperials would have had to have permission from the empire to stage a coup."

"And so they did," Risilan said. "Malbeck promised to increase the output of bioweapons by several millions of tons per year if they allowed him to make his attempt. The empire gave their approval."

"And you've similarly asked the empire to let you do this?" Jason asked.

"No," Risilan replied. "I haven't bothered. Because there is nothing I can offer them. Especially considering I intend to shut down bioweapon production entirely."

Jason stared at her. He didn't know what to say. She was an idealist. But it sounded to him like she was putting her entire population at risk for those ideals.

"You think I'm a fraud, don't you?" Risilan said.

"Not at all," Jason lied.

"Yes, I can tell," Risilan said. "We Tyrnari can read micro expressions. I've studied thousands of your avatars over the years, knowing that someday I might make an alliance with humanity. I know how to interpret those micro expressions. You're laughing at me, inside."

"I just think you could be putting your people in a whole lot of trouble," Jason said.

"Trust me, my people approve of my plans," Risilan said. "They don't want to be part of this empire. They don't want their homeworld to be used to produce bioweapons for that empire's army. Just as you don't want that for your world."

Jason nodded. "You have a point, there."

"My people will fight if they have to," Risilan said. "Some will prefer that we remain under the yoke of the empire, yes. But the majority want freedom."

"Maybe you should have a vote on it," Jason said.

Risilan stared at him, and then laughed aloud. "Ah,

you humans can be so entertaining. But I think I've had my fill for now. Until next time..."

She vanished.

"Well, that was interesting." Jason stood up and stretched his legs. Then he returned to reality and continued the march in his mech form.

12

J ason and his army marched for the next four hours until Jhagan called a halt.

"Why are we stopping?" Jason asked. He gazed between the tree trunks ahead to confirm the Modlenth army had halted as well.

"Scouts have detected an Imperial patrol," Jhagan said. "Risilan plans to remain here for the next three hours."

"Why three hours?" Jason said. "Once they've gone past, we could wait fifteen minutes to make sure they're not coming back, and then continue on our way."

"It's not as easy as that," Jhagan said. "Usually, patrols return the same way they've come. Certainly, we will be long gone by the time the patrol returns, but we'll have left behind ample evidence of our passage. When the patrol see the depressions and tracks we've made, they'll alert the city."

"All right, team, looks like we're resting for a few more hours," Jason said.

Jason assumed a comfortable standing position, and then ran through the Damage Report sheets of his army. All units were thoroughly repaired by now; one tank had been destroyed for spare parts, but otherwise the army had suffered no further losses since leaving the Modlenth city.

He received a private call.

It was Iris.

"What can I do for you?" Jason said.

"We have a dinner date," Iris said.

"What?" Jason said.

"At eight o'clock, remember?" Iris said.

"Oh... yeah."

"And since we're stuck here anyway, I'm going to hold you to it," Iris said.

Jason sighed. "I'm not really in the mood for——"

"I don't care if you're in the mood or not," Iris said. "I've spent the past hour cooking Baqala polow for you, and you're going to eat it."

"What?" Jason said. "It doesn't take that long to cook in VR."

"Yes, but it takes that long to prepare the proper imagery, texture and taste," Iris said. "I had to accelerate my timebase to the maximum, you know. Just for you. Many days have passed for me in that hour. Days spent getting this recipe just right. You're not going to refuse me. You wouldn't dare!"

"All right," Jason said. "Guess I'm entering VR. Z, would you mind taking control of the mech?"

"Gladly," Z said. "Have fun! Let me know if you want me to join you. I kind of like her."

"Uh, maybe next time," Jason said.

He signed out of reality and switched to his VR loading screen. Once more he created a duplicate of his partition, and logged into the copy for some privacy.

He stood in the kitchen.

He accepted the VR entry request from Iris, and she appeared a moment later. The Middle Eastern woman was dressed in her usual pink shawl, matched to a demure black dress that ended above the ankles. She was wearing sandals. Her face seemed exceptionally bronzed today, and she had overdone it a bit on the eye shadow—it looked like she'd been punched in either eye. Still, he wasn't going to complain: she was sexy no matter what she did with her makeup. Definitely a far cry from the six-legged and four-armed Locust mech she piloted.

She was holding a tray containing a big pot and two plates. She set it down on the table and grabbed some utensils from the cupboard.

Jason sat down, and she took a place opposite him.

She caught him staring at her eyes. "I've overdone my eye shadow, haven't I?"

"Not at all," Jason lied.

"I look like a drag queen with two black eyes," Iris said.

"No, no," Jason said.

Instantly the eye shadow vanished. "How's this?"

"Just as good," Jason said. *Much better.*

She smiled, and scooped some rice from the pot into her plate. Jason did the same, and then dove in.

"Mm, this is good," Jason said.

Iris nodded, smiling. She swallowed. "Baqala polow is rice with fava beans and dill weed."

Jason nearly choked on the rice he was in the process of swallowing. He got it down, and then said, in a bit of a squeak: "Dill weed? Good choice of dish."

"I thought you'd like it," Iris said, giving him a flirtatious look. "I love eating dill."

He swallowed nervously.

"By the way," Iris continued, the seductive tone leaving her voice. "I just wanted you to know, I don't have sex on the first date."

Ah. So that was what she was playing at.

Jason was very familiar with this game.

"Good, because neither do I," Jason said as casually as he could manage.

She looked up. "Really?"

"Uh huh," Jason said. "I don't have sex on the first date. Sorry."

"Oh," Iris said. She seemed disappointed.

Jason couldn't help but smile inside. He knew how to turn the tables on these girls quite easily by now. They'd trained him very well.

Even so, he wasn't going to press for sex. In truth, he wasn't really in the mood. Not with a fight coming in a few hours. And try as he might, he couldn't get thoughts of that battle out of his mind. Nor his meeting with Risilan, earlier.

Iris seemed to pick up on his troubled thoughts,

because she asked: "Have you met Risilan in your VR yet?"

"I have, actually," Jason said.

"How was she?"

"Weird," Jason told her.

"That's all you have to say?" Iris said.

"Well, basically, I'm not sure we can trust her."

"Of course you can't trust her," Iris said. "She's an alien. I don't believe for a minute that she's going to send us back."

"Well, if she doesn't, then we'll take the city back from her," Jason said. "And then force her to return us to Earth. Or figure out how to do it ourselves."

"You always make things sound so easy," Iris said. "It'll be more complicated than that."

"I know," Jason said. "It always is. But I like to break things down into simpler, easier to understand chunks first. It's what I've always done. Something I learned back in my professional gamer days."

"You were a professional gamer?" Iris said.

"Uh huh."

"No shiyat," Iris said. "So was I. Ever heard of Team Electron?"

"Nope," Jason said.

"They were my sponsors," Iris said. "After I signed with them, I moved into a mansion in Houston and gamed full time. They paid me a salary of four thousand creds a month. Meals were included. Every day, breakfast, lunch, and supper were prepared by professional chefs. We had a personal trainer take us into the weight room after breakfast. After workout was personal time, and then lunch. After that, from noon until six we played. Then we had dinner until seven. And played again from seven to one A.M."

"Wow, sounds like a sweatshop to me," Jason said.

"Depends on your point of view," Iris said. "If you're doing something you love, and getting paid a very decent wage, you can't call a job a sweatshop."

"Maybe," Jason said. "What happened?"

"Well, I'm sure you know, there's a lot of turnover in the professional gaming industry," Iris said. "I got kicked off Team Electron after four months, and was between sponsors. That's when I decided to get a mind scan done, for some extra creds. And here I am."

"Nice," Jason said. "I was never invited to join a team. Well I mean, I had sponsors, but they weren't the all-inclusive sort, like yours. And yeah, I was essentially between sponsors when I got my mind scanned, too."

"Interesting," Iris said, taking another scoopful of rice. They ate in silence a moment. "We talked about not being able to trust the alien. But you're not really sure you can trust all of the other girls either, are you? Given what Aria and Xin did…"

Jason put down his utensils, swallowed, and regarded her uncertainly. "Trying to sow dissent?"

Iris shrugged, smiling innocently. "All I'm saying is: maybe you'd be better off trusting those of us who've never betrayed you."

"Like you?" Jason said.

She merely continued to smile.

"I should remind you, you did attack me, when we

first met," Jason said. "Along with Maeran and Cheyanne."

"That was a misunderstanding," Iris said. "We were still enslaved to Bokerov. Besides, I heard we weren't the first to attack you. Tara did so as well. We have fought well for you, since then, haven't we? Haven't I?"

Jason pursed his lips, and nodded ever so slightly. "You have."

"Good," Iris said. Her eyes glittered with self-satisfaction, as if she'd made some really important point. Or at least, one that was important to her.

Motion drew Jason's gaze to the kitchen entryway. He saw blond hair, a freckled face. A long tail curving around the doorframe.

Lori was peaking in.

"How did you get in here?" Jason said. "This is a private partition…"

Lori shrugged. "I have my ways."

Her nonchalant answer made him wonder how private his past partitioned sessions had been. Had she watched every one of them?

Lori stepped inside completely. "Hi Iris!"

"Oh hi, Lori," Iris said. Disappointment momentarily flashed across her face, but she masked it quickly. "Would you like to join us?"

"Sure!" Lori said.

Again the disappointment appeared, but this time Iris made no effort to hide it.

Lori grabbed a plate and utensils from the cupboard and sat down beside Jason. She squished her thigh against his as she served herself, and kept it there as she tried the rice.

"Mmm," Lori said. "I really love the digital flavors! This is amazing."

Iris smiled in appreciation. "Thank you."

The smiled dropped when Lori set down her utensils and wrapped her arm around the crook of Jason's elbow: a sign of ownership. At least, that was how Jason interpreted the gesture. She pressed her cheek against his shoulder and sighed.

"I wish this were real," Lori said. "All of this. You, me, Iris. Alone in a house beside a mountain lake. That there was no alternate reality we could step into, a reality where we were trapped on an alien homeworld, potentially marching to our deaths to help some alien princess we know nothing about."

"She met Jason," Iris said. "In VR."

Lori pulled away from him to look into his eyes. "Really? What did she say?"

Jason shook his head. "Nothing special. She told me a sob story of her youth, how she listened to the screams of her family dying. How she wants vengeance."

"Oh," Lori said. She tried some more of the rice. "This is really good." Then she added, casually: "Did you fuck her?"

Jason froze. "Who?"

"Risilan," Lori said.

"No," Jason said quickly. "Of course not."

"Then why do you sound so guilty?" Lori said. "Like I caught you with your hand in the cookie jar?"

"Because your question took me by surprise, especially that you'd ask it in front of Iris," Jason said. Though the truth was, it was more guilt over the fact that he *wanted* to have sex with Risilan's avatar, more than anything else. But he wasn't about to tell Lori that.

Z appeared, dressed in her white wetsuit. "He's just embarrassed because he wanted to have sex with Risilan."

"Z!" Jason said. "Damn it. Stop reading my mind!" He deactivated the Accomp, and she vanished entirely.

"Oh, that's all it was?" Lori smiled. "Okay then." She wrapped her arm around his elbow again, and snuggled against his side. "I don't mind you having sexual transactions with the other Mind Refurbs. But an alien? That's where I draw the line."

"Are you sure it's not just because she's a princess?" Iris said.

Lori shifted against Jason, but didn't answer.

"Why would she care if Risilan was a princess?" Jason said.

"The same reason I do," Iris said. "She's the only one who could tempt you away from us."

"That would never happen," Jason said.

"Are you sure?" Iris said. "What if she offered to allow you to rule at her side? Giving you control of her planet? Her space navy?"

Jason felt his brows draw together. "Never happen. First of all, she'd never make the offer. Second of all, I wouldn't accept. I have my own homeworld already. My own girls."

Iris shrugged. "So you say now."

"Stay away from the princess," Lori said softly. "Can you do that for me?"

Jason looked at her, and saw those innocent eyes looking imploringly into his. "As long as you promise not to invade my private VR partitions anymore."

Her eyes twinkled slightly. "Done! Thank you." Lori gave him a kiss on the lips, and then vanished.

"Well, that was… rude," Iris said.

"You did invite her," Jason said.

"Yes, but the polite thing to do was decline," Iris said. "This is our dinner date, after all. And this was a private VR partition, right?"

"That's right," Jason said.

"There you go," Iris said. "She was doubly rude for intruding on that. You should punish her."

"I'm not like Bokerov," Jason said.

"I'm not saying do anything major," Iris said. "Her punishment can be as simple as denying her sex."

Jason frowned. "That sounds like more of a punishment for me than anything else."

"Well you get where I'm going with this though, right?" Iris said. "You take away privileges she's earned, until she learns to obey. You have to keep your people in line…"

"If she does it again, I'll do something," Jason said. "Until then, I'm going to trust that she'll keep her word."

Iris shrugged. "If that's what you want."

They didn't talk about much else during the date. Jason finished his plate, and he was trying to decide whether he should switch seats so he could kiss Iris goodbye, when she stood.

"Well, I thank you for the date," Iris said. "Maybe we can do this again sometime."

"Wait." Jason pointed at his cheek. "Kiss goodbye."

She hesitated, then leaned forward to press her lips against his cheek. At the last moment, he turned his head so that she pecked his mouth instead. Her eyes widened, and she pulled back.

"Nice trick," Iris said.

"Wasn't a trick," Jason said.

"Shut up." She leaned forward again and kissed him even more passionately.

Jason really got into it, matching his mouth movements to hers, and he also reached up to squeeze her breast behind her dress.

Iris abruptly pulled away.

"Something to hold you until next time," Iris said.

"I want you now," Jason said.

"But you don't have sex on the first date, remember?" she said sweetly.

And with that, she vanished.

Damn it.

He hadn't turned the tables on her after all. She'd gotten the upper hand.

It was just as well: he'd completely forgotten about the coming battle with that kiss, but it all came flooding back.

Time to get to work.

13

———

J ason stood with his army on the outskirts of the Imperial-owned city. They hadn't yet emerged from the forest, whose eaves ended about one kilometer away from the base of the dome, but they were already taking fire from the city. In between the eaves of the forest and the city wall was a no man's land full of fallen Imperial troops—the fleeing scouts and patrols that Jason's army and the Modlenth battalion with him had harried all the way here. Jason had tried to avoid those patrols for as long as he could, but eventually it became impossible, given the size of his army, and thus ensued the long chase to his current position.

The Imperial city was bigger than the Modlenth one. A lot bigger, at least judging from the ring-like wall that encircled the place and generated the energy dome, as well as the size of that dome itself, which literally reached to the heavens. That dome, in addition to keeping out the atmosphere, was also seemingly impervious to every type of weapon: sometimes a shot from the Modlenth went astray, striking the dome, but it simply absorbed the impact. Jhagan had told him that hitting the dome with weaponry only made it stronger.

Jason and his army had positioned on the west side of the city, as per Risilan's plan. Jhagan was with him, along with a hundred other Modlenth mechs, two hundred elliptical aircraft, and ten airships. Jhagan had agreed to share positional data with him, so Jason could see all the members of the Modlenth battalion on his overhead map, regardless of whether they were in view of any of Jason's units or not. He could also see any enemy targets that weren't visible to his own units, targets that showed up as a plethora of red dots along the western side of the city.

The airships were at the front, just inside the ring of trees, and were taking the brunt of the attacks from the many turrets that lined the city wall. Elliptical Imperial craft also fired plasma and energy bolts from where they had deployed along the outside of the dome.

The combined armies returned fire, targeting those turrets. At least those that had a view of the targets. The Modlenth mechs, as well as the War Forgers and their clones, had spread out along the eaves of the forest, and employed the trees as shields while they aimed past the thick trunks. The elliptical aircraft were also spaced between the upper branches of the trees, using them for cover as they fired.

Meanwhile, Bokerov's tanks fired shells that arced skyward and plunged toward the city walls, using visual data fed to them by the War Forgers. The shell attack wouldn't last for very long, however, as the tanks were low on ammunition. They'd have to switch to their renewable plasma bolt attacks soon, but that could only happen when they moved forward and obtained a direct line of sight upon their targets.

The Cataphracts at the rear remained hidden beneath the treetops, waiting their turn to strike.

Shaggy was just beside Jason, behind the tree, with a leash around his neck that was pegged to the ground. The Rex Wolf fought frantically against the restraint, wanting nothing more than to break free and join the battle. Bruiser and Lackey were similarly restrained behind a trunk near Tara, while Runt was with Lori.

"Easy, boy," Jason said. "You'll get your chance, soon."

Operating in Bullet Time, Jason switched to the scope of his laser and aimed at one of the turrets that protruded from the distant wall. He fired. The glow of an energy shield lit up around the target, fading a moment later. He kept firing, keeping his main vision active in a corner of his display for peripheral awareness.

After the fifth strike, the energy shield no longer activated. But before he could deliver the death blow, his attention was drawn to his main visual feed, where an energy bolt was homing in on him. He pulled back behind the tree as a portion of the trunk dissolved beside him.

Close one.

What would I do without Bullet Time?

With Z's help he calculated the source of that bolt.

It was one of the Imperial craft in the sky next to the dome. He leaned out, and targeted that craft next. It, too, was shielded, and he had to pull back as it fired another energy bolt at him.

Beside him, the airships with his army fired lightning, energy, and plasma bolts as their ramps opened, and the specially designed bioweapons deployed. The creatures dashed forward, exultant at their newfound freedom, and drawn by the bright flashy lights coming from the wall.

They were essentially elephants minus the trunks, with big bony plates covering their heads and upper flanks. Those plates weren't entirely natural—they'd been augmented with Modlenth tech. The beasts also carried autonomous lasers on their backs, as well as energy shield generators, and explosives.

"Pack Mules!" Lori said.

"Your alien names are the worst," Sophie said.

Most of the defensive turrets redirected their fire toward the incoming bioweapons, which were obviously deemed the greater threat at the moment, so that the airships were no longer under such heavy bombardment. Even so, one of the more damaged airships went down as Jason watched, crashing into the no man's land next to the forest.

While that was taking place, Jason saw four new targets appear on his overhead map. His eyes were drawn to them, because they were moving fast. Too fast for ground units.

He glanced skyward, and spotted four dots he guessed were bombers. He zoomed in. These aircraft had the same elliptical shape as the others, except they possessed large rectangular sections underneath. Definitely bombers of some kind.

And they were on a bombing run.

Several of the Modlenth craft swooped skyward to intercept it.

Jason returned his attention to the battle at hand. He had to trust that those intercepting craft would be able to deal with the bombers.

When the first group of Pack Mules reached the wall, proximity sensors triggered the explosives they carried, carving huge blast craters in the surface when they exploded. More and more creatures were drawn to the same portion of damaged wall—likely steered by the chemical signature of the dying bioweapons, just as bees were drawn to the death of drones when the hive was under attack.

Several fireworks ignited in the sky above as the bombers were taken out by the craft he had seen take to the skies moments before.

"How long do we have until the Imperials move their space navy into firing range?" Jason asked.

When that happened, the battle would definitely be over. For the Modlenth.

"Risilan tells me we have half an hour," Jhagan said.

"Half an hour?" Jason said. "We were supposed to have a two hour window!"

"Yes," Jhagan said. "But apparently the warships were a lot closer than we thought, with several already in orbit. Be glad it's not a two minute window!"

"They've breached the wall!" Tara shouted over the comm.

Jason glanced at the wall at the base of the dome. The Pack Mules had indeed breached the wall, and were pouring into the gaping hole the exploding bodies of their companions had drilled. The bioweapons were dropping like flies on the other side, however, as they were killed by whatever was waiting within—their shields had obviously been drained by the enemy turrets on the way to the opening, and hadn't been able to take much more.

Directly above the breach, a large sliver had been cut out of the energy dome, representing that portion of the protective shield the lost wall section had generated. Yellow mist flooded inside. Jason wasn't too worried about what would happen to the alien residents: Risilan had assured him that by now any civilians would have evacuated to specially designed structures meant to be used during a shield failure, where they would be protected when the toxic atmosphere flooded in.

"I hope all the innocents made it safely inside their shelters!" Lori said.

"I don't!" Bokerov cackled.

"Forward," Jhagan ordered.

There were a hell of a lot of turrets still active on those walls. Not to mention enemy flyers… the Imperials would have a field day shooting them down. Then again, if they delayed to take down more of those turrets, the enemy might seal the breach, allowing the space navy to arrive. In fact, he could already see what could only be repair drones lining the ragged upper edges of the gap. They moved fast, replenishing the damaged materials, smoothing out the inner surfaces.

Through his scope, Jason aimed at one of those drones with his energy weapon, and fired. He watched with some satisfaction as it dropped.

"Forward, War Forgers!" Jason said. "Bokerov, fill in the gaps along the tree line with your tanks. Try to give us as much cover as you can. Send the Cataphracts forward as well. Stick to the tree line when all your troops are in place, and wait for my order to come inside."

Bokerov sighed. "As you wish. But why do you always get to have all the fun?"

"We have the mechs," Jason said. He untied Shaggy. "Let loose the dogs of war!"

I've always wanted to say that.

As Jason ran into the no man's land between the eaves of the forest and the gap in the wall, he considered giving the order to combine, but that would just make his War Forgers a bigger target for the defense turrets fired from the wall, and the enemy flyers. Plus it would make passing through the gap more difficult— they'd have to sidestep past, leaving them vulnerable until through.

Shaggy ran at his side. The Rex Wolf moved at a sprint, forcing Jason to up his servomotors to match his speed. He was operating in Bullet Time of course.

Aria was directly in front of him, and she had deployed her shield to protect herself from the incoming fire. The others formed up in a line behind Jason.

The other War Forgers used similarly formations.

The Modlenth mechs, half the size of Jason's War Forgers, crossed the field in one big square formation. That formation wasn't particularly synchronized, and there were gaps throughout as some of the units tripped, or fell from the incoming fire. The Modlenth flyers swooped low, moving inward toward the missing slice of the energy dome. The airships also accelerated forward, firing the whole time.

As Jason and his War Forgers closed with the wall, their flanks were exposed to the turrets on the far left and right sides of the wall ahead, not to mention to the flyers overhead.

Sophie adjusted her speed and activated her shield as necessary to deflect any bolts that came in from the sides. Maeran backed her up, redirecting her three drones to form shields with their connected energy beams.

Jason opened fire at some of those turrets that were within his line of sight. Shields no longer flashed into place—most had already been worn down—and he was able to take down a few. He also occasionally fired at the flyers overhead, but wasn't able to penetrate their armor, at least not with his laser.

His War Forgers reached the breach and flooded inside ahead of the Modlenth mechs; they leaped over the dead bodies of the bioweapons. The street beyond was made of that translucent material layered over a gold substrate.

The Arias formed a defensive half-circle in front of him, interlocking their shields side by side. The rest of the War Forgers and their clones huddled behind those shields, which were turning red on the inside as the units took heavy fire.

The Modlenth poured in from behind; some of the half-size mechs took cover behind the War Forgers, others immediately fanned out, firing at targets Jason hadn't yet seen.

In the air behind him, the airships weren't able to fit through the thin sliver that had been cut in the energy field, so they remained in place there, simply firing through the opening. The airships also targeted the different repair drones that were attempting to restore the gap at the base of the dome.

Jason hadn't deployed his Explorer—he was too worried about it getting shot down. However, Jhagan had given Jason read access to the camera feeds of the flyers, so Jason tapped into one that was darting overhead as part of the strike force. The video image moved back and forth as the flyer zig-zagged to evade the incoming fire, but he simply accelerated his time sense to the max to get a freeze frame, allowing him a bird's eye view of the area beyond the breach.

On the opposite side of the street, the buildings began: large, gold, triangular things. Those buildings were about two stories tall here on the outskirts of the city—just a little taller than the mechs—and grew successfully taller toward the city center, just like in the Modlenth city.

The War Forgers were located in the middle of the street beyond the breech. Between the buildings across from them, and behind them, were a series of Phaser mechs. There were also hundreds of elliptical flyers, positioned at various points in the sky. Both air and ground troops were unleashing a steady barrage of weapons fire, battering the shields the Arias held.

Suspended in midair he saw a missile, moving toward the central Aria: his.

"Aria," Jason transmitted. "You got a missile headed straight toward you."

"I see it," Aria replied, her timebase automatically syncing with his own. "I'm going to have to pivot out of the way, ladies. So, if you don't want to get hit by that missile, I suggest you do the same."

"Are you sure it's not a seeker?" Tara said.

"I guess we'll find out shortly," Aria said. "I'm launching my Battle Cloak, too."

14

Jason amped up his servomotor output and switched his time sense to something more manageable; time was still slowed, but at least he was no longer frozen. The missile was also incoming a whole lot faster.

Aria fired her Battle Cloak, and tiny seekers erupted from the nozzles that circled her mech. The missile didn't change course to target the tiny objects, which were actively swerving to intercept the missile.

"Don't think it's a seeker," Aria said.

She leaped into the air, lifting her shield and spinning her torso out of the way at the same time. Jason meanwhile swiveled his hips to the side, toward Jerry, who was making room for him; the missile traveled underneath Aria, and passed where Jason was just standing. One of the Battle Cloak seekers struck the missile then, and the device detonated.

A black blob expanded outward from the impact site, reaching toward Jason and the others.

"Ah shit, it's one of those," Aria said.

Jason was still dodging outward in Bullet Time. Behind him, Lori and the others were also doing their best to get out of the way.

Jason promptly hit another mech—Jerry, who was trapped in turn by John beside him.

"John, we need some legroom here!" Jerry said.

John gave up some space, and Aria 2 moved with him so that he remained protected by her shield, but that meant said shield was no longer joined to Aria 5 immediately beside her. Aria 5 was also on the move, to keep Jerry protected.

Aria was falling straight back down, directly into the path of the expanding blob. Jason reached out and grabbed her foot, yanking her along with him as he continued into the space that Jerry freed up.

That black blob expanded outward, and part of Aria's left arm was struck by the substance as she fell, but Jason pulled her free from most of it.

She hit the street, and Jason still dragged her, causing sparks to rise where her mech met the translucent top.

"That's good," Aria said.

The blob had ceased expanding, and now simply hovered in place, searching for targets.

During that time, Jason and Aria were still pummeled by plasma and energy bolts, and their armor had taken damage. Everything was still working however.

For now.

Jason increased time a little and Aria clambered to her feet, restoring the shield to its previous position. The black blob meanwhile floated toward her.

"Time to assume defense positions behind the nearby buildings!" Jason said. "Aria, take the Originals to this building." Jason marked off one of the structures next to the street. "Other clones, choose your targets!"

"Can I come in, yet?" Bokerov sent.

"Not yet," Jason replied.

Aria dashed forward, heading toward the building Jason had marked off. Jason stayed close behind her, along with the other members of the Originals; they moved at a crouch.

Jason fired past the edges of the shield, striking a Phaser with his railgun, and then following up with an energy attack as it phased back in.

He'd lost sight of the Rex Wolves, but then a growling up ahead alerted him to Shaggy's position: the Rex Wolf had a flyer in its mouth, pinned to the ground as it worried the craft. The elliptical fuselage abruptly caved, crushing the shell.

Nearby, Bruiser had an Imperial mech pinned— apparently this one hadn't phased out.

"Not all of them are Phasers," Aria said.

"I noticed," Jason said.

Jason scanned for the other Rex Wolves, but had to duck as a plasma bolt nearly nailed him in the head. He stayed low, keeping behind Aria's shield from then on. The Wolves were on their own for the moment.

Behind him, in the middle of the street, another

missile exploded. The black goo enveloped two Modlenth mechs, and they toppled to the street, their black forms shattering entirely upon impact.

"Um, there are enemies clogging the streets on either side of the buildings ahead!" Aria said. "It won't be much cover."

"Clear them!" Jason said.

Cheyanne threw her two blades forward. One blade struck an Imperial mech, the other a Phaser; the latter unit phased out, and her sword embedded into the surprised Phaser just behind it. She recalled the blades, and they returned to her metal palms while she was still on the move.

"Cover me," Cheyanne said. She moved her wings in a blur, and arced upward from the rear of the column. Enemy fire began to follow her.

But then Xin immediately flared her hull, and leaped forward, spinning like a drill toward the enemy.

Aria fired her lightning bolt weapon over her shield.

Tara teleported forward; she stabbed a Phaser and it immediately vanished from this reality, she swung her sword to the side, striking an Imperial mech and taking it down, then withdrew the sword and plunged it into the Phaser's cockpit just as the mech rematerialized. She moved through the enemy chopping away.

Sophie launched her micro machines, Maeran her drones. Iris struck out with her energy whips. Lori had become invisible, and according to the overhead map, it looked like she was trying to sneak behind enemy lines.

Xin plowed into the closest Imperial mechs, melting portions of their hulls. Some phased out.

Cheyanne landed among the tangos who were firing from between the two buildings up ahead, and she began rotating like a spinning top, her swords chopping into every enemy around her. Using her invisibility, Lori pushed unready mechs into those swords; she also fired the plasma bolt from her tail at any tangos that attempted to target the relatively exposed Cheyanne.

Other mechs and flyers continued to target Aria and her shield, which was almost dissolved as she took cover behind the triangular building. The other Originals had cleared out the closest enemy mechs that had been firing from between the structures, allowing Jason and the others to deploy behind the buildings and use them as cover in turn.

Jason glanced at the other nearby buildings and saw that the War Forger clones had similarly removed the closest enemies, allowing them to take similar cover behind the golden structures lining the street. The Modlenth mechs were with them, and were slowly pushing forward. As far as Jason could tell, all of the Modlenth flyers had been shot down. There were still some airships firing from the opening in the energy dome, however.

Jason gazed past the edge of his current building, toward the city center. There were enemy mechs hiding behind the different triangular buildings up ahead. The Phasers unleashed lightning bolts from their swords, and other Imperial mechs launched energy bolts and blob missiles from mounts on their forearms.

On the empty streets between the buildings, he could see the bodies of the dead bioweapons that had been mowed down as they tried to race deeper into the city.

Overhead, the enemy flyers continued to unleash hell down at the group. Their numbers hadn't really been reduced all that much. Jason had to duck as energy bolts came at him from a couple of those flyers, and the edge of the triangular structure dissolved beside him.

"We have to take down some of those flyers!" Jason said.

"Maybe Cheyanne can fly up there and do her spinning top thingy," Lori suggested.

"Are you kidding?" Cheyanne said. "I'll be shot down before I even get close."

The Sophies launched their micro machines, and had them move evasively to avoid taking fire as much as possible. The micro machines struck the different flyers, and rotated like a saw, slowly cutting through the fuselages. It usually only took a few seconds to penetrate, at which point the flyer would fall from the sky.

Meanwhile Jason and the others unloaded at the craft, dropping as many as they could. When they hit the street below, they often struck other enemy mechs that were lying in wait.

"When can I come inside?" Bokerov said. "Why do you always get to have all the fun? And have you forgotten that the space navy is going to arrive any minute now?"

"It hasn't been half an hour yet…" Jason said.

"No," Bokerov said. "But that estimate could be wrong."

"Eliminate as many turrets as you can along the wall over the next five minutes," Jason said. "I'll send you an update, then. We're trying to clear you a path in here."

"But I don't *want* a path cleared!" Bokerov said. "I want to be the one clearing the path!"

"You'll get your chance soon enough," Jason said.

He ducked as several more bolts struck his position, and lost more of the triangular building.

"Should we combine?" Julian said.

"Not yet," Jason said. "With all those flyers still out there, we'll just make ourselves more vulnerable. Jhagan, where the hell's the diversionary attack?"

"Coming," Jhagan said.

"He sounds like a waiter at a restaurant," Cheyanne said. "When you ask where the food is, while you're starving meanwhile!"

"Except this time we're not starving," Tara said. "We're fighting for our fucking lives!"

"That's my point!" Cheyanne said.

And then most of the enemy flyers abruptly turned around and fled to the east. According to the overhead map, they weren't headed toward the city center, but rather making a beeline to the far side of the city.

"Well look at that," Jerry said. "The princess finally decided to send in the second strike force."

"They overcommitted air troops to this side," Jhagan said. "It's an easy mistake to make. But reports are coming in from the second battalion that there are just as many mechs, if not more, gathering beyond the eastern energy dome, where they've begun the second assault."

Jason nodded. That made sense, because none of the enemy group troops had broken from their current positions.

"Bokerov, now you can come," Jason said.

The next few minutes were spent trying to push forward; both attackers and defenders were essentially pinned in place. Sometimes the Phasers used their abilities to reposition on the far side of the building, or when Tara regained enough charge, she teleported, but otherwise, there was very little troop movement.

And then the tanks and Cataphracts arrived. The tanks poured through the opening, moving into position next to the triangular buildings and firing out into the streets beyond, further pinning the enemy units.

The Cataphracts, meanwhile, had to slowly squeeze through the thin opening, sidestepping. Since the units were so big that they overtopped the outlying buildings, Jason and the others had to provide covering fire.

Once they were through, the big guys began unleashing hell.

"Watch and learn, combiners!" Bokerov said.

The Axeman swung down with that huge axe of his, biting through buildings and the mechs hidden behind them. The Lizardman fired a huge energy beam from its mouth that cut through the triangular structures and toppled them. The Octopus ripped buildings away with its tentacles, revealing the enemies beyond. The Cobra struck out at those enemies, crunching down on them with its mouth. The Rifleman launched the huge energy cannon he carried in his arms. The Caterpillar latched onto opponents and cut through them with the powerful laser cutter built into its maw.

"You know, we can probably join in the fun now that the flyers are gone…" Jerry said.

"You're starting to sound like Bokerov," John said.

"You're asking to combine?" Jason asked.

"I am," Jerry replied.

"Go ahead, clones," Jason said.

The different clones began to race toward their respective Arias as the male Mind Refurbs initiated the combine process.

Jason was about to initiate his own transform when Lori's status indicator turned a dark red. He glanced toward her position. She had been sneaking behind enemies lines, still invisible, but one of the Phasers had caught her apparently, because its sword was protruding from her chest assembly.

It had stabbed the weapon right through her torso, and into her battery area, deactivating her, and returning her to the visual band. Meanwhile her body was seizuring as electrical currents sparked up and down her hull.

The Phaser withdrew the sword and Lori's mech dropped to its knees, inactive, motionless. The Phaser drew back the sword to attempt another strike—this time the blade was lined up with her AI core.

If that sword struck, everything that made Lori who she was would cease to exist.

15

"Lori!" Jason said.

He had already lined his weapon up with her attacker, and he unleashed an energy bolt.

The Phaser responded by winking out of existence. Jason dashed into the street, knowing full well he was putting himself into harm's way, and yet not giving a damn.

When one second had passed since his last shot, he fired another energy bolt, and it struck the Phaser two hundred and fifty milliseconds later, just as it phased back into existence. The bolt disintegrated half the sword, and plowed into the mech's body, carving a big blast hole that sent the Phaser offline. It toppled to its knees beside Lori.

Other mechs hidden behind the buildings on either side were opening fire at Jason, but he continued racing past in Bullet Time. The other War Forgers did their best to offer him covering fire, as did the Cataphracts, but he still took a couple of good hits: one bolt plowed into his side, nearly eating through his armor all the way to his main battery. Another struck his swivel mount, disabling the laser.

He reached Lori, scooped her up, and continued deeper until he was past the wave of defenders embedded between the buildings. Then he promptly turned into a side street, and took cover. He lowered Lori's mech to the street beside him.

He would have been panting from the exertion were he human.

He peered past the building edge and saw that the combined War Forger clones, along with the Cataphracts, were making short work of the remaining defenders. Jason's Originals joined them in their attack, along with Iris, Maeran and Cheyanne. He spotted the four Rex Wolves, which were continuing their attack against the enemy units. The wolves were covered in blood—it had to be their own. The sight made Jason feel sick. He hoped the animals weren't too badly injured. They'd taken wounds before during different hunts, and usually healed relatively quickly. Still, he was worried by what he saw...

"Do you need help?" Aria asked.

"Negative," Jason said. "I'll camp out here until you guys are finished, then we can reunite. I don't want any of you risking your lives in another 'run of death' like the one I just made. The dogs might need your help, though. It looks like they're covered in blood."

"*What?*" Tara finished her current target and cut her way toward the dogs. She went to Bruiser and slid a metallic hand across his hide. The animal snarled at her in surprise, and nearly attacked until he realized who it was.

"That's not blood," Tara said. "It's sweat, you ass. Don't do that to me!"

Jason slumped in relief. "It looked like blood from here."

"That's just because their fur is damp," Tara said. She checked the other three mutants just to be safe, and then continued to fight, staying close to the dogs.

Jason waited where he was, keeping an eye on his surroundings for any potential ambushers. This included continually scanning the sky above, and the rooftops of the nearby buildings, which were slightly taller here.

He occasionally glanced toward the west to observe the progress of his army and the Modlenth battalion with them, and also toward the far Eastern side, where the second Modlenth battalion was only just breaking through the dome on that flank. Now that he was away from the fighting, he could hear the klaxon that was blaring throughout the city.

His attention was drawn northward by a bright flash of light. A hole had been drilled into the base of the dome there by some sort of bomb.

He zoomed in and saw Modlenth mechs and flyers swooping inside. It was the final group led by Risilan herself. They would make their way to the palace near the center of the city, and once there, Risilan would retake the throne.

That was the theory, anyway.

The third group vanished from view beyond the many interceding buildings. But even though Jason wasn't able to see them with his eyes, he could still gauge their progress because their positions updated on his overhead map,

He continued checking for signs of any ambushers around him, while glancing occasionally at the map; he watched as Risilan's group stopped next to a building near the city's center. It had to be the palace Risilan was looking for.

As he continued to look at the map, he realized that the group was no longer moving. They had assumed positions around the perimeter, and didn't budge.

Something was wrong.

A moment later the units began to turn black—they were going down.

"Jhagan, has Risilan reached the palace?" Jason asked.

"She has," Jhagan replied. "It looks like the Central is in some trouble! We're going to have to divert. Keep your army here!"

The Modlenth mechs stopped firing at the targets still entrenched behind the buildings around them, and began racing toward the city center. The Imperials fired at their backs, while Jason's army in turn attacked theirs.

"At least bring along a few of my Cataphracts," Jason said.

"They'll be vulnerable to the palace defenses, if those defenses haven't been shut down," Jhagan said. "Stay here and guard against any reinforcements the space navy sends!"

"I thought there were limits on how big of an army the empire allows its member species to keep?" Jason said.

"There are!" Jhagan said. "The troops aboard the warships are included in that limit."

Jhagan and the surviving Modlenth mechs pulled away from the fighting near the breach, and continued toward the city center.

Jason glanced at his overhead map, only to see more of Risilan troops turn black next to the palace. None of the other units with her had moved.

"I'm going to join Jhagan," Jason told Bokerov and his War Forgers. "Stay here, and guard our left flank!"

"What about Lori?" Tara asked.

"I'm taking her core with me." Jason was already opening up Lori's damaged chest panel; he retrieved the cylinder that contained the AI core and slid it into his storage compartment. Then he abandoned her mech. If the Imperials found her, they could do whatever they wanted to the body: her mind was safe.

At least, as long as he didn't take a wound to his storage compartment.

Maybe I should have stowed her AI core between some buildings or something.

He dismissed the thought and ran on.

A moment later Tara landed at his side. "Buddy system."

Jason nodded reluctantly. "What about the dogs?"

"They'll be fine," Tara said. "They've grown, in case you hadn't noticed. Not just physically."

Aria arrived next, then Xin, Sophie, and Cheyanne.

The latter two sprinted in a side street that ran parallel to his own.

He was okay with one or two arriving, but almost his whole team?

"I told you to stay!" Jason said. "You could have been shot down getting here!"

"We're not scared of the run of death," Iris said, appearing in another side street with Maeran. "If the princess fails, we all fail."

Jason glanced at his rear view camera feed and confirmed the combined clones were staying behind, along with the Cataphracts, and tanks.

"At least some people know how to obey orders," Jason complained.

He reached the rear of the Modlenth battalion that was led by Jhagan.

"I told you to remain," Jhagan transmitted.

Jason felt suddenly embarrassed: he had only just been chastening his War Forgers about the ability to obey orders...

"Most of my army remains behind," Jason said, stumbling over his words slightly. "I figured the princess could use the help."

When Jhagan didn't answer, Jason took the silence for approval.

The buildings grew successively taller around him as Jason neared the city core. The group faced no resistance along the way. It seemed that all of the troops were occupied at the three main combat areas: the western and eastern breaches, and the palace.

When the battalion was completely surrounded by

skyscrapers, Jhagan took a southern turn, heading toward the palace—as indicated on the overhead map —from a side street. After a block, the towering buildings receded, revealing a neighborhood whose triangular structures were only a little higher than Jason. Any units larger than Jason and his War Forgers would have been exposed above those shorter buildings. It was probably a good thing the Cataphracts and combined mechs had stayed behind.

Ahead, the palace came into view. It reminded him of the residence Risilan used in the Modlenth city: four towering walls that were slightly bigger than his mech, with triangular towers thrusting from each of the four corners. He couldn't see the courtyard beyond, but the top portion of the inner building was readily visible—it was a pyramid of some kind.

Ahead, Modlenth mechs from the third strike group had taken cover behind various buildings close to the palace perimeter: one of them had the topknot that marked Risilan's bodyguard. That meant the princess herself was somewhere among them.

Turrets fired relentlessly from the palace walls, and forced the survivors of the Modlenth battalion with Jason to shelter behind vacant buildings. There were several flyers hovering over the palace that also joined in the defense.

The War Forgers took cover as well.

"Good of you to show up," Risilan said over the comm band. Voice only.

"We said we'd fight…" Jason aimed his energy weapon past the edge of the triangular building he used for cover. He fired at a turret that protruded from the outer wall of the palace.

A convex field flashed into existence a meter in front of the wall and absorbed the blow. At first he thought it was a localized energy field protecting the turret, like those that had shielded the turrets of the main dome, but something seemed off about the shape of that field. It was too flat. More fields flashed into existence as the War Forgers targeted different turrets, but they too all had that same flat shape. Jason aimed above the turret, at a bare portion of the wall, and unleashed another shot. That area was protected, too. He realized the entire palace was covered in an invisible energy dome.

"What happened to your 'friends' embedded inside the Imperial palace?" Jason said.

"They weren't able to disable the defenses," Risilan said.

"Well that puts a crimp on things," Jason said. "Jhagan, how do we lower the energy dome from the outside?"

"We don't!" Jhagan replied.

Jason was still in contact with those members of his army who had remained near the breach, thanks to the scouts Jhagan had dispersed throughout the city to act as repeaters. So when Jerry sent a transmission, Jason received it right away.

"We're under attack by reinforcements," Jerry said. "Looks like the space navy finally sent down some transport ships."

"If they were smart, they'd shut down the city's

entire energy dome and just open fire on us directly from orbit," Julian said.

"Oh no, they can't do that," John said. "They don't want to harm any of their buildings. Preserving their cultural heritage and all that."

"Why do I feel like I'm talking to myself?" Jason commented.

"Probably because you are," Jones said.

Jason glanced at his overhead map and saw countless red dots appearing outside both the western and eastern breaches in the main city wall. There were probably more troops entering from the northern section, but apparently any scouts Risilan had left behind to watch that third particular breach had ceased transmitting. Reinforcements were also likely flowing inside from unmarked entrances, and would soon outflank Jason's army, and the Modlenth.

They were running out of time.

16

Jason was considering their options when Tara spoke.

"I can teleport inside," Tara said. "I just need to recharge for a little while."

"And once you're through, then what?" Jason said. "You'll be exposed on all sides."

"I did something similar at Bokerov's base," Tara said.

"This isn't Bokerov's base," Jason said. "You go in there, you'll draw fire from every unit. You won't survive."

"But I might be able to take down the defensive shield before I do," Tara said.

"What if she took someone with her?" Aria said. "Tara, I thought you had the ability to teleport one of us, too?"

"I can," Tara said. "But I'll have to recharge a lot longer."

Jason shook his head. He switched to a private band to exclude Jhagan, who would have heard everything else. "It's still too risky. Especially considering that we don't know if this Risilan will keep her word. I won't have any of you sacrifice yourselves for her."

"You're talking about the teleport technology used by the Banthar?" Jhagan interjected.

"Er, yeah," Jason said, returning to the main comm band. He didn't want to admit that humanity had stolen the tech from the Banthar, but it looked like Jhagan had already guessed as much.

"Then it won't work," Jhagan said. "The teleportation equipment can't form a fix through an energy field."

"There you go," Jason told Tara.

"Sappers," Sophie said.

"What?" Jason said.

"Cover me," Sophie said.

Sophie left the protection of her building and raced into the street toward the palace.

It wasn't really possible to cover her from the turrets, which were shielded behind the palace's main defense field, so the War Forgers and Modlenth mechs concentrated their fire on the enemy flyers overhead.

"Aria, with me!" Jason got up and dashed forward, following Sophie. He wasn't going to let her do whatever it was she planned alone.

Turrets in the palace wall launched plasma and lightning bolts at Sophie, but her personal energy field still had enough charge to protect her. That field saved Jason, too, because he was right behind her. Aria piled in behind him, and held her pocked shield overhead to protect him and her from any flyer attacks.

"Sophie, you're heading straight for the energy dome!" Jason said.

Sophie ignored him, racing forward. The attacks from the embedded turrets picked up. Sophie's energy shield failed. Bolts tore into her armor, but she continued onward. Jason was hit by a few, too— evidently the weapons required a recharge interval to fire at full capacity, because these blows only caused a fraction of the damage he would have expected. That made sense, considering that the turrets had been firing nonstop since his arrival. Still, if that pounding kept up, Sophie wouldn't last much longer. Especially if she stunned her mech by plowing into the energy dome.

"Sophie!" Jason said.

She dodged to the left at the last moment, diving behind the building that was the closest to the palace—a wide triangular structure that could fit three mechs. She crunched over the wreckage of several Modlenth mechs that had fallen there.

Jason joined her, as did Aria, who deployed her cratered shield like an umbrella above them. The trio were safe from the turrets embedded in the palace wall, thanks to the building, but those flyers were the greatest threat at the moment, especially considering that previous plasma and energy attacks had taken a toll on the shield: there were several large holes along the edges, with smaller gaps in the inner regions. Jason doubted it would last much longer.

"Risilan, War Forgers, keep the flyers occupied, please!" Jason said.

"What are you planning?" Risilan said.

"You'll see," Jason said. He glanced at Sophie. "I hope you know what you're doing."

Sophie's avatar gave him a smile with the teeth bared. "While I was once a social media star, I'm now an advanced war machine capable of limitless death and destruction. So yes, I know what I'm doing."

"Famous last words," Aria commented.

The War Forgers and Modlenth concentrated their attacks on the overhead flyers, drawing most of the fire.

Sophie meanwhile formed her micro machines into a large drill and sent them spinning into the triangular building beside her. The machines focused on the bottom of the wall and broke through after several moments.

She waited while the micro machines enlarged the gap, and then Sophie lowered her body to the street, forcing Jason and Aria to make space. She peered inside.

"There are rooms in the way," Sophie announced. She reached in with one arm and punched several times, then looked through the opening once again. "This will do."

He switched to her viewpoint and watched as she directed her micro machines through the smashed inner walls and toward the far side of the building; when they arrived, they swooped downward, and began drilling into the floor.

"You're digging a tunnel underneath the palace walls, and the energy dome?" Jason said.

"Like I told you, sappers," Sophie said.

"The palace turrets have begun firing on the building," Aria said. "So far it's holding up. Not sure how long it will last."

"If it becomes compromised, we'll move to the next building," Jason said, nodding toward the adjacent triangular tower nearby. Sophie would still have control of her micro machines at that distance.

He hoped.

It took her ten minutes to tunnel underneath the energy dome, the palace wall, and into the courtyard beyond. The passage was extremely tight and narrow, not big enough to fit even a human being—not that they had any humans with them.

But that wasn't who the tunnel was designed for.

Sophie sent her micro machines inside.

"Can you see with them?" Jason asked.

"I can organize some of the machines into camera systems," Sophie said. "Mounting them atop weapons and other objects I might form."

As she spoke, the point of view he'd tapped into changed—a camera had formed atop her micro machines, which had taken the form of a spear-like weapon.

Mechs and defense turrets inside the courtyard were opening fire at the flying weapon.

Sophie separated the machines like a pro to avoid the strikes, and then recombined them when the threat passed. She kept the camera intact through it all, maintaining the viewpoint.

"You're like a Phaser mech without the phasing," Aria commented, also evidently viewing the feed.

"Risilan, describe the energy field generator for me," Jason said.

"It will look like a cylinder, protruding from the ground," Risilan said. "Green pulses travel up and down various channels carved into the surface. The top will look like an unfolding Resna."

"A what?" Jason said.

"A flow," Risilan clarified. "It should be somewhere near the center of the courtyard."

Sophie steered her combined micro machines between the smaller outbuildings, occasionally separating them to avoid a plasma or energy bolt. She plunged the spear formed by the machines into a few Imperial defense platforms along the way, destroying them.

"There!" Jason said, spotting the generator in question.

"I see it," Sophie said.

The spear backtracked, turning toward a tall cylinder that was precisely as Risilan had described. It was surrounded by eight Phaser mechs who stood in a tight circle around it, swords in hand.

Sophie separated the micro machines into their constituent parts and flew the individual machines, and the camera, past the defenders, who sliced down with their swords, or shot lightning bolts from the weapons.

They struck some of the machines, but not enough to make a difference.

Once past them, Sophie swiveled the micro machines around the cylinder, forming a maelstrom of cutting knives, and began tightening them, grinding down the generator. In moments the pulses of green light that ran up and down the grooves along its length grew dim.

Jason leaned past his cover and released an energy bolt at a nearby turret on the palace wall. His weapon penetrated.

"The localized dome is down," Jason said.

The Modlenth mechs began to open fire on the turrets, and disintegrated several of them.

"Charge!" Risilan said.

The Modlenth mechs flooded into the street and raced toward the entrance. The main doors were sealed, but they didn't care: those in the forefront simply knelt, while those that followed used them as steps to leap over the wall.

Jason and his War Forgers took down as many turrets as possible, and then joined the Modlenth, like-wise using the kneeling mechs as stepping stones.

By the time Jason got inside, the Modlenth had already destroyed most of the Imperial mechs and their defense platforms.

He terminated some of the remaining units, helping Jhagan secure the courtyard. Meanwhile Risilan and her personal guard charged the palace itself. He knew it was her group, because he saw the mech with the topknot among them.

The fighting ended shortly thereafter, and the remaining forces surrendered, including those sent by the space navy.

The king attempted to flee in a large elliptical transport, but the Modlenth shot it down. It crashed in the street a few blocks from the palace. Risilan and her personal guard dragged the emperor and his family from the wreckage. The royal family members weren't wearing protective suits, and their alien bodies immediately showed signs of distress—tentacles flailed about, abdomen sacs crimped and puckered. It was obvious Risilan intended to let them die from exposure to the toxic atmosphere that had flooded the city.

"We don't have to watch this," Jason said, turning his back on the grim sight. "Our work here is done."

"If she doesn't send us home, she's going to suffer the same fate," Tara commented.

JASON LOITERED with the rest of his army along the western perimeter of the city, just inside the city wall. If Risilan betrayed him, he felt it was best to be close to the exit. Then again, that exit was quickly closing up as Tyrnari repair drones mended the breach in the city wall.

Speaking of repair drones, Jason and his army had their own drones at work. Any spare materials they needed were taken from the wreckages of tanks that were beyond repair.

"How many of these tanks contain your actual

consciousness?" Jason asked Bokerov. "Versus being under remote control by one of your clones?"

"One in ten," Bokerov said. "Well, except for the bigger tanks. And the Cataphracts. Each of those contains a version of me."

"Interesting," Jason said. "So the platoon of tanks you gave Aria, was it all autonomous units?"

"No," Bokerov said. "I gave her one clone of my consciousness to command the group. The rest are autonomous."

Lori's mech was soon repaired, and Aria replaced the battery with a fresh power cell taken from a lost tank. Jason then installed her AI core into the unit.

The Stalker clambered to its feet.

"What happened?" Lori said. "It's over?"

"Yes," Jason said. "We won."

"I was hit… I'm sorry!" Lori said.

"Doesn't matter," Jason said.

"What happened?" Lori pressed.

"I'll fill you in later," Jason said.

Repairs continued for the next few hours; by then the energy dome breaches were completely sealed, and Jason and his army were trapped inside. The yellow mist was being vented out so that the citizenry could return to their daily lives. Tara lounged just outside the walls with the Rex Wolves, who wouldn't be able to survive the native Tyrnari atmosphere—neither of the double lungs each mutant possessed supported that environment.

"I don't like all this waiting," Cheyanne said. Her

avatar bit her lips. "What's taking the alien so long to live up to her end of the bargain?"

"Apparently they're confirming her as empress," Jason said. "She won't have control of the rift generator until then."

"Or so she claims," Cheyanne said.

After a few minutes a large delegation from the Imperial palace finally appeared. A contingent of Modlenth mechs, leading Imperial mechs whose arms were bound by energy ropes. One of the mechs had the familiar white topknot, indicating the royal guard, and Risilan's presence among them.

"Risilan, are you out there?" Jason asked over the comm band.

"I am here," Risilan said. "I'll speak with you in a moment. There are some prisoners I have to release, first."

The group halted a block away from Jason's army, and then the Modlenth released the Imperials they had captured. The mechs seemed surprised at first, but then they ran to the base of the energy dome, and began to leap over it, right through the enclosing field itself.

"How are they able to pass through the energy dome?" Jason asked.

Jhagan was the one who answered. "We are able to adjust sections of the energy dome to allow them to pass through, by momentarily disabling the defensive component of the field but leaving the atmospheric membrane in place."

Jason nodded. "When we were attacking earlier, the defending Imperials should have just let us through.

Instead of allowing us to make a breach, and having the toxic atmosphere flow inside."

"Maybe," Jhagan said. "Then again, the citizenry would have evacuated the streets either way."

Jason watched the prisoners make a run for the eaves of the forest a kilometer away from the city. He kept expecting the turrets that lined the exterior walls to open fire and mow them down.

But as the fleeing mechs reached the forest and vanished inside unharmed, Jason said: "You actually didn't kill them, Risilan. I'm almost surprised."

"My two hearts aren't made of stone," Risilan said. "These prisoners refused to denounce the Imperials and follow me as their Empress. Of course they could not stay, but rather than execute them, I chose leniency. Besides, none of them were members of the royal family, and thus did not deserve death."

"Where will they go?" Jason said. "Will other cities welcome exiles like these?"

"No," Jhagan said. "But they're headed to the northeast, where one of the smaller rift stations is located. It's one we haven't yet secured."

"So wait, what are you saying?" Jason asked. "They're going to Earth?"

"That's right," Jhagan said.

"Let them tell the other Imperials what we've done," Risilan said.

"The prince might surrender," Jhagan said. "If you promise to exile him."

"He won't," Risilan said. "I won't make such a promise anyway. I want him dead."

"What prince?" Jason said.

"He leads the army the former king sent to Earth," Risilan said. "Prince Amadan, last member of the Imperial royal family."

"You claimed his army would return?" Jason said. "And attempt to take the city?"

"That's right," Risilan said. "They will leave your Earth behind."

"How?" Jason said. "Through one of the smaller rift stations you mentioned? That aren't in your control?"

"Those are too small for his army, but it doesn't matter," Risilan said. "Prince Amadan has taken rift generators to Earth with him."

"Ah," Jason said.

"But none of this concerns you in any case," Risilan said. "You're going, remember?"

"Well, it does concern me, because I want to make sure Earth is safe," Jason said. "If this Amadan doesn't return his army, we'll have to do some prodding."

"Oh, he won't need prodding," Risilan said. "When he learns the throne has fallen, and that his family is no more, he and his army will arrive well before you are gone."

"Why?" Jason said. "Can't you send us sooner?"

"I'm sorry, but for an army your size, you'll have to proceed onto the plains, to the staging area where you first arrived," Risilan said. "That is where the rift will be created. When you have reached the spot, I will know, and will open the gateway to your planet."

"You should have told me earlier that it was so far

outside the city," Jason said. "My army could have been making its way already."

"Yes," Risilan said. "My apologies. I guess I entertained a small hope you would stay."

"Why would I stay?" Jason said.

She didn't answer.

"What if I run into the incoming Imperials?" Jason said. "Led by this Prince Amadan?"

"Then avoid them," Risilan said. "But chances are, you won't even see them. As I told you, they will create their own rift."

"All right, thank you," Jason said.

And he left.

17

So it was done. Jason had helped conquer the city for Risilan, and now he could go home.

Assuming Risilan kept up her end of the bargain.

Jason wasn't entirely convinced that the Imperial army would be gone when he reached Earth. The smart thing to do would be for this Prince Amadan to stay on Earth and create as many new troops as he could before returning.

Then again, vengeance could be a strong motivator. It could even have been the strongest driving force for these Tyrnari, whose minds no doubt worked at least somewhat differently than humans.

Also, it was advantageous to strike now, while Risilan was newly crowned; her army had suffered big losses during the taking of the dome, and the Imperials she had released would report that to Amadan.

Ah well, with luck, when he got back to Earth, it wouldn't be his problem. He could focus on shoring up his mountain base against any incursions from the humans into his territory. It was funny: once he got back, humanity would probably be his biggest problem.

Jason had put Z in control during the walk through the alien forest, with instructions to wake him if he was needed. With luck, they'd reach the rift site without running into any roving bands of Tyrnari bioweapons. Or Prince Amadan's army.

Jason was in his personalized VR, of course. He'd just finished free climbing to the top of one of the mountains that bordered the lake. He'd never climbed this one before: it was one of the more difficult mountains, and the route he chosen was definitely more technical than what he was used to, but he'd pulled it off.

And now he was simply lying there, basking shirtless in the sun; because of the way the crest sloped downward, he was able to observe the distant lake below. It was about the size of a thumbnail. His house was just a dot next to that lake.

He felt a furry tail wrapping around his chest.

"Hey Lori," Jason said.

"Tickle, tickle, tickle!" Lori said. Her tail moved up and down his ribcage, but he didn't react.

"You know, it's funny, in real life I was ticklish," Jason said. "But as an AI core, not so much. The peripheral nervous system code probably needs some tweaking."

"I'll have to look into fixing that!" Lori said as she lowered herself to lounge beside him. "Because I can't not be able to tickle you when I want to!"

Jason smiled at her. Her blond hair seemed so bright

in the sun, and her freckles redder, giving her such a cute girl next door look. "You're looking energetic today."

She was leaning on her elbows, like him, with her legs stretched out in front. "Tara told me everything that happened. I feel so bad that I missed it. And ooh, that queen is so evil. She killed the whole royal family by dragging them out of the wreckage of their escape ship, and then letting them dissolve in that crappy atmosphere!"

"She did," Jason said.

"If you were in her shoes, you wouldn't have done that, would you?" Lori said. "Just to secure a stupid throne?"

"Hmm," Jason said. "Well, I would have killed the emperor for sure. But you're right, I probably wouldn't have had the heart to kill the entire royal family. I'd probably have to jail them though, for the rest of their lives, to stop them from eventually overthrowing me."

"Death might almost be preferable, given that option!" Lori said.

"Maybe, maybe not," Jason said. "I'd give them full access to VR, so even though they were prisoners in body, at least their minds would be free. There would be no access to the Tyrnari Internet equivalent, of course."

Lori nodded, then gazed at the surrounding peaks.

"I feel so bad about getting hit," Lori said after a moment. "Just when you were probably getting ready to combine."

"Nothing you could do," Jason said.

She glanced at him. "You're not mad at me?"

"Of course not," Jason said.

"Thank you!" She gave him a quick hug, followed by a peck on the cheek before she pulled back. "So, I wanted to let you know…"

"Yes?" Jason said.

She abruptly reddened, and looked away. She gazed at her feet, and wiggled her toes. "Look at my toenails! Do you like the designs?"

She'd painted little pictures of Runt on her toenails.

"Yes, it's pretty sweet," Jason said. "So what did you want to let me know?"

She sighed. "Oh, nothing. Well I like you, you know that right?" She was looking at him again. Into his eyes.

"Well, yeah," Jason said. "And I like you, too, obviously."

"Any chance we could ever tie the knot?" she said quickly. Then looked away.

"Oh," Jason said.

"Ah, sorry," Lori said. "I shouldn't have said that."

"No, I applaud you for speaking your mind, rather than holding it in," Jason said. He paused, and gazed out at the lake. "I'm not at a point in my life where I'm ready to settle down. Especially not with one person. I—"

"Oh, it would be an open marriage!" Lori said. "I'm happy just being your wife."

Jason had to shake his head at that. "Think for a moment on the jealousy you'd inflict on the other girls. The envy. You think Sophie treats you badly now? Just think what she'd do if I announced I was marrying you."

Lori frowned, then looked away.

"Look, we're machines," Jason said.

"No," Lori said. "You're always telling us that we're human!"

"Not exactly," Jason said.

"You have, too," Lori said. "I have recordings!"

"What I'm trying to say is, we can't follow the conventions that normal humans follow," Jason said. "It doesn't suit our present situation. Just like monogamy doesn't. There's really no point in getting married, other than to draw attention to you, so I'm sorry, I'm going to have to say no. I don't want to play favorites among any of the girls."

"Ah, that's it, then," Lori said. "You want to keep your options open, huh? Want to keep your steady stream of harem girls coming to your bed."

"That bed isn't even real," Jason said. "Nor is any of this."

"But it *feels* real," Lori said. "And that's all that matters."

"Maybe so," Jason said. "But I still can't marry you."

Her eyes teared up, and her lip quivered, but she quickly looked away.

Jason sighed. "I'm sorry." He tried to rest a hand on her shoulders, but she yanked from his grasp. "You're still my favorite."

"Yeah, sure," Lori said angrily.

"Lori—" he began.

"If only I hadn't been shot," Lori interrupted. "I

ruined the last mission… I wanted to shine, be the hero. If I had, you would've said yes."

"No, I wouldn't have," Jason said.

"I'm going to go," Lori said.

"No," Jason said. "Please don't. You can't leave, not like this. We need to be good."

She wiped at her eyes, and when she looked at him, she forced a smile. "We are good."

"No, we're not," he said slowly. "I love you."

She seemed stunned. "Do you mean it?"

"Yes," Jason said.

She hugged him very tightly. "I love you, too! So much!"

"But I also love the other girls," Jason said.

She released him, and pulled back. "Oh. I knew there was a catch."

"You're all like family to me," Jason said. "Without you, I wouldn't know what to do. I would have probably died in the uninhabited zone, attacked in my sleep by a Nightmare. Or of loneliness, anyway. Or maybe I would have become like Bokerov…"

"Somehow I can't imagine you as bat shit crazy," Lori said. "Hm. Then again, maybe I can."

"Thanks," Jason said.

She grabbed his hand, and squeezed. Then she looked into his eyes: "Thanks for telling me how you feel. It means a lot to me. I don't want to force you to choose any one of us. I don't know why I brought it up. I guess, after almost dying back there, it reminded me of how precious life is. And I wanted to marry you before it was too late. But I realize, I don't have to. I'm happy just having you by my side. I'm happy sharing you with the others."

"All right," Jason said. "Thank you for understanding."

"I still expect you to come to my bed first every night, though," Lori said.

"We've been alternating…" Jason said. "You one night, Tara the next."

"Yes, Tara and I have talked," Lori said. "If you're going to start sleeping with everyone else, this rotation thing isn't going to work."

"I don't think I can stand to have sex so many times a night," Jason said.

"Why, it's not like your equipment is going to fail," Lori said.

Jason nodded. "True. But I mean psychologically. I'll start getting your names mixed up in bed. And that'll earn me a few slaps."

"More than a slap, I'm sure," Lori said. "Well, okay fine, I guess we'll keep the rotation thing for now. But I'm not sure it's going to work long-term."

"I'm not sure any of this is going to work long-term," Jason said. "I've been taking it one day at a time."

"That's somehow not very reassuring," Lori said. She sat up. "I'm going to go now. Oh, by the way, I hear the dojo is ready. You might want to visit Aria and Xin."

With that, she vanished.

Well, he figured he might as well check it out while he waited to reach the rift.

He teleported to the forest clearing that Aria and

Xin had been using. Sure enough, a Japanese-style building resided before him. Essentially a pagoda, it had two tiers of curving tile roofs nestled one atop the other, with the topmost slightly smaller than the lower roof. The walls were made of wooden panels.

Xin was standing next to the entrance. She was wearing a kimono with a colorful sash.

She bowed wordlessly when she saw him, and held out an arm, gesturing toward the entrance.

"Impressive," Jason said.

She maintained her bow, waiting for him to enter.

Jason walked inside.

Within, he found a small arena of sorts. A large sparring mat lay in the center of the hardwood floor.

Aria was waiting on the opposite side of the mat. She looked all vampire today with that pale face and red lips. She even had the fangs. She was dressed in a white karate outfit. Her belt was brown.

"Brown, isn't that the second most proficient, after black?" Jason asked her.

Aria merely held her arms out in front of her, and clasped her hands, then bowed.

She wants to fight, does she?

Jason approached the mat. "Neither of you are going to say a word to me?"

Aria continued her bow, as if waiting.

Jason transformed his clothing to match her white robes. The belt he wore was also white. "Go easy on me. I know nothing about karate."

Well, that wasn't entirely true. He had some

Training AIs that could teach him everything he needed to know.

He pulled up his HUD, and activated Z in hidden mode.

"Hey Z," Jason thought. "I need you to take over my VR avatar. Looks like I'm going to have a sparring match with Aria, and I don't want to embarrass myself too badly."

"You want to cheat?" Z said. Her avatar appeared on his HUD, visible to his eyes only. She waved an admonishing finger. "Tsk, tsk, tsk."

"It's not cheating," Jason thought. "It's leveling the playing field."

"I don't think I can help you with this," Z said. "Sorry."

"What?" Jason thought. "You're my Accomp! You have to do what I say."

"I like these girls too much," Z said. "I'm afraid you're on your own."

With that, her avatar vanished from his HUD.

Shit.

"Whining about it won't change anything," Z's disembodied voice said in his head.

He shut Z down entirely.

Aria was still bowing, hands crunched in front of her; Jason mimicked the gesture, and then she assumed a defensive pose.

"This is stupid," Jason said. He walked up to her. "Go ahead, beat me up. I can't do anything."

"At least try to defend yourself," Aria said.

"She speaks!" Jason said.

Aria's fist came flying in. Jason dodged to the side, but was too slow; the fist pounded him in the jaw.

Next thing he knew, he was on the mat. He scrambled to his feet, rubbing his jaw.

Aria came in again.

This time she swept her foot along the floor, tripping him, and he was lying on the mat once more.

Over the next minute, she constantly knocked him down. Sometimes with her feet, sometimes her hands. He pulled up his Training AI in the background, and ran through some techniques in another VR partition in Bullet Time. That helped a little, but not much.

Finally Aria stepped back; Jason lay panting on the ground, while Aria hadn't even worked up a sweat.

"All right, are you done making me your punching bag yet?" Jason said.

"That felt really good." Aria smiled. "Xin? Your turn."

Xin entered, and when he saw the hungry look on her face, he slumped. Her kimono had transformed into a karate outfit.

"Ah, shit," Jason said.

He did a little better, thanks to the moves he was absorbing in the other VR partition, but in the end she still kicked his ass. It was obvious by then that both of the girls had dialed up their strength settings, because he should have been able to catch some of those blows. He didn't amp up his own settings in return—he figured he'd give them this one chance to kick his ass. Because the next time he came down here, he'd be wearing a black belt, he swore.

So once more he found himself lying panting on the mat, with Xin hovering above him, untouched, and breathing normally. She offered him a hand. Jason took it, and she helps him to his feet.

"Thank you for that," Xin said. She glanced at Aria. "This was a great idea."

"Did you guys really build this by hand?" Jason said, examining the space around him.

"Mostly," Aria said. "We did resort to some digital touch-ups, to make it perfect."

"All right, so I guess you've finally forgiven me for my earlier gaffe about you guys showing me loyalty?" Jason said.

Xin nodded.

"Seems like you spent a lot of work to build something that you'll only ever use once," Jason said.

"Oh don't worry, we'll bring you back here when you make your next mistake," Xin said.

"Great, I get to look forward to an ass kicking each time, huh?" Jason said. "I have to warn you, next time I won't be so easy. I'll be trained up, and ready."

"We look forward to it," Xin said.

Aria stood beside Xin, and licked her lips as she looked down at him. "Why does he seem so cute when he's lying there defenseless like that."

Aria opened up the black belt at her waist, and then opened up her robe and untied her pants, letting both fall to the ground. She was completely naked.

Xin did the same beside her.

"Oh, crap," Jason said.

"Make up sex?" Aria asked.

He teleported them to a private VR partition, duplicating the dojo. Then he had sex with the two of them right there on the mat. He even kept his anatomy the same this time, trying out different positions he'd thought of. They worked like a charm.

He lay back between them when it was done. He was going to be very careful with what he said.

"Thank you," Aria said.

"You're welcome," Jason said.

"Oh, not for the sex," Aria said. "But for being who you are."

"That's a compliment, I guess," Jason said.

"Yes," Aria said. "We could have been trapped here with any other man. Instead, we got you. I used to pine for my husband. I've completely forgotten him, thanks to you." Her gaze became distant, pained.

"You haven't forgotten the children, though," Jason said.

"No," Aria said.

Xin rubbed her arm. "We're here for you."

"I know," Aria said. She smiled at Xin. "You've helped me forget my old life, too. Honestly, I can't imagine going back."

There was still a slight sadness to her voice, and Jason knew her words weren't entirely true.

He decided to try changing the subject. Jason rubbed his neck, and when he removed his hand, he saw blood on his fingers. "Why did you have to draw my blood during sex?"

"I dunno, I thought you'd like it," Aria said. She still had her vampire fangs grown out.

"It certainly turned me on watching you do that," Xin said.

"You would get turned on from that," Jason said.

She shrugged.

"So we're almost home," Aria said.

"Don't jinx it," Jason said.

"Oh, we'll make it, I'm sure," Aria said. "Believe it or not, I'll kind of miss this place. Earth, and humanity... well, they don't really mean as much to me anymore. Because truthfully, we take our real homes with us, up here." She tapped her head. Then she gestured to the dojo. "This is our true home, now. And it doesn't even matter where our robot bodies are physically. At least not to me."

"I'd have to agree with that," Xin told him. "If you decided to stay here, on this world, I wouldn't actually mind. We could explore the planet, document the different bioweapons, and enjoy our lives inside VR in between doing that."

"She's right," Aria said. "Think about it, we'd be safe. Under the protection of a queen who rules the entire planet. We wouldn't have to worry about humanity one day trying to capture or destroy us."

"Assuming she took us in," Jason said. "And doesn't betray us. And also assuming that she survives whatever attack this Prince Amadan makes. And the eventual assault from the empire."

"We could help her in the defense of the planet," Xin said. "Further securing our position high in her favor."

"Or we could simply take the planet for ourselves," Aria said. "Depose her, and make you king."

Jason glanced between the two of them in disbelief, and then he sat back, chuckling.

"Why do I get the sense that you two planned all of this?" Jason said. "As part of some attempt to convince me to stay?"

Xin snuggled against his left side, while Aria did the same on his right. They both traced finger patterns across his chest.

"Maybe we did," Aria said. "But you can't say you didn't like our attempts to convince you."

"You're right at that," Jason said. "But we are going back. We'll be safe on Earth. That's where we belong. We'll work out a treaty with the humans, somehow. I know we will."

"All right," Aria said. "Whatever you say, Boss."

Jason looked at her. "I like it when you call me Boss."

Aria grinned seductively. "You also like it when I do this."

He definitely liked what she did next. And he took the two of them all over again.

18

Jason advanced near the head of his army.

Shaggy walked close to his side, limping slightly. The animal had injured one leg, and Jason had formed a splint out of two spare rods and a canopy one of the tanks had carried. Runt had a similar splint, while Bruiser and Lackey only suffered superficial cuts and scrapes from the battle. They were in relatively good spirits—in addition to the life-giving sunlight that constantly shone down from the sky, Jason and the others had fed them some of the spare meat from their storage compartments. It was a reward for fighting so well.

They were still in that sprawling forest whose trees reached well above their mechs, including the Cataphracts; he had yet to reach the region containing the smaller pine trees, closer to the rift. According to his overhead map, he still had quite a distance to go before the trees transitioned. His Explorer traveled near the forefront of the group, and acted as a scout, keeping that map updated. The Modlenth were not with them: they had stayed behind to protect the city from the coming attack that was expected when the prince returned.

There were still a few units undergoing repairs among Jason's army. Dismantled tanks were dragged along at the rear of the army for spare parts.

As he marched, Jason received a call request from Bokerov on a private line and accepted.

"Hey, Shit Eater," Bokerov said.

"Don't call me that," Jason said.

"Come to my VR," Bokerov said.

"Why?" Jason said.

"You want to see what I look like, don't you?" Bokerov said.

"Not particularly," Jason said.

"Just come," Bokerov said. "You'll want to see this."

"You're up to something…" Jason said.

"*Nyet*," Bokerov said. "I am a good boy, as you Americans like to say."

Jason muted Bokerov, and looped in Lori.

"Hey, Babe!" Lori said. "What is it?"

"Bokerov wants me to enter his VR," Jason said.

"Why?" Lori said.

"He doesn't want to say."

"I'd avoid it," Lori said. "It's possible he figured out how I cracked his VR code, and he wants to do the same to you."

"That's what I thought," Jason said. He unmuted

Bokerov, and muted Lori in turn. "Sorry, Bokerov. I'm staying where I am."

"That's all right, I got everything I needed from you," Bokerov said, and immediately closed the line.

He unmuted Lori. "What the hell is he up to? Did you detect anything usual in the data packets he sent my way, or vice versa from my end?"

"No," Lori said. "Everything seems fine. Maybe he's just trolling you?"

"That's a possibility," Jason said. "I want you to keep an eye on him. Watch out for any strange transmissions. And if you can, grab his activity log from the past twenty-four hours."

"The former is easy, the latter, not so much," Lori said. "I left a bunch of my own backdoors in his code after I escalated my privileges, but he's closed them all up. So it's going to take some time."

"Can't you force him to re-open them?" Jason said. "We have Containment Code control over his mind, after all."

"It's not as easy as that," Lori said. "Things like software patches aren't covered by Containment Code. We can order him to rollback those changes, but he can veto the request if he wants. And I can't force him to send me his activity logs, because he doesn't have any. He claims he turned off logging. I've already ordered him to turn it back on. But some sort of activity log should still be stored in a backup subsystem, one that his conscious mind wouldn't have access to. Which is why I say it's going to take me some time to get those logs."

"Do what you can," Jason told her. "And take whatever precautions you can. I don't want you exposing your own code to him. Last thing we need is him taking over your AI core in a fight."

"Don't worry about me," Lori said. "I can hack my way out of any sandbox. For the most part."

She disconnected.

Jason continued the march. He was considering going back to his VR, if only for a break from the monotony, when his Explorer sent an alert.

He glanced at the overhead map, and saw that five red dots had appeared, moving above the treetops.

"Tangos sighted!" Jason said.

As he watched, more dots appeared as the Explorer detected others, so that in moments there were forty-three of them.

Jason zoomed in on the objects using the Explorer's camera. He spotted white, elliptical shaped aircraft.

"We've got alien flyers," Jason said.

"Imperial?" Sophie asked.

"That's my guess," Jason said.

"That was fast," Tara commented. "The queen was right about the Imperials wanting payback."

"Or maybe it's just power they thirst for," Iris said. "They want to attack now while Risilan's army is still weak."

Jason recalled his drone and had it fly just below the tree line. "Just our luck that their rift happens to materialize in our path."

"Maybe it's not luck," Tara said. "Maybe Risilan knew they'd return this way, via the original rift site."

"She told me it was random," Jason said.

"But that's exactly my point," Tara said. "It might not be. Maybe she hopes that by sending us this way, we'll buy her some time."

"She wouldn't sacrifice us like this!" Lori said.

"Oh?" Tara said. "How can you be so sure? None of us really know this queen very well. She could be the meanest bitch in the galaxy for all we know."

"Wait, have the aliens seen us?" Jerry asked.

"Don't think so," Jason replied. "Which is why we're changing directions immediately. Heading south, perpendicular to the direction of those scouts. Bokerov, turn your Cataphracts and tanks to the south. Same with the tanks under your command, Aria. The rest of you, with me."

Jason turned to the south, but before he had walked three paces, the Rex Wolves abruptly darted west into the trees.

"No!" Jason said. "Tara, catch the dogs!"

"Bruiser!" Tara shouted. She teleported ahead, grabbing onto the scruff of Bruiser's neck, but it was too late to catch Runt, Shaggy, and Lackey: they vanished into the undergrowth.

"Damn it," Jason said.

He spun west. "Originals, with me! Clones, stay here with Bokerov."

Jason darted forward, and he'd gone maybe ten meters when the Rex Wolves returned. They dove through the undergrowth, appearing beside Tara, who still had Bruiser.

Jason heard a crunching sound behind them.

And then towering, four-legged beasts burst through

the undergrowth. They vaguely resembled huge rhinoc-eroses because of their thick, folded skin, except their heads were small nubs containing a single big eye, and they lacked horns of any kind. They carried weapon turrets slung over their backs so that they were like armed gunships.

"Looks like the Imperials have been augmenting their army since they left!" Aria said.

"Rhinoeyes!" Lori said.

"You and your wacky names," Maeran said.

Since Tara was the closest, she immediately attacked. She stepped to the side and swung her sword down, cutting off the small nub the lead Rhinoeye used for a head. The eye, along with that head, dropped to the ground. Blood squirted from the injury, but the animal blindly ran on.

Tara leaped behind the thick trunk of a tree as the weapon turrets of other Rhinoeyes opened fire on her.

As the other creatures raced past her, they too opened fire, this time targeting the other War Forgers. Different Arias swung their ballistic shields into place. The Sophies activated their localized energy fields. Maeran launched her three drones and formed a shield in front of herself.

The rest of the War Forgers and their clones took cover behind the different Sophies and Arias, or nearby trees.

Jason chose a tree trunk for himself.

He waited for an animal to rush past beside him, and then unleashed his energy weapon. The beam tore into its side, cutting a wide gash that caused organs to jut out from within. Rather disgusting, really.

But the animal kept running.

"Sturdy things," Jerry commented.

Aria opened fire with the tank platoon assigned to her. At least Jason assumed the tanks were hers, because they would be the closest to the party. Plasma bolts and energy beams erupted from the turrets, drilling into the creatures. Some of the animals plowed right into her tanks, which weren't able to move out of the way fast enough, and either rammed them, flipping them over, or fired their own turrets.

The enemy flyers began to swoop down as the aircraft in the vanguard arrived.

Jason decided to target them, as they were the immediate threat: the Rhinoeyes seemed intent on simply charging forward, and hitting whatever lay in their path. Bokerov would have to deal with them.

Jason heightened his time sense and aimed his weapon at a flyer, which was about as big as his chest plate, and fired. An energy shield kicked in. They were more like the flyers he had faced in the Imperial city, rather than those he had dealt with on Earth. That wasn't good. Not at all.

"They've got upgrades!" Jason said.

Because of the shielding, he unleashed his railgun, too. He switched to his laser, which was less draining on his battery, and fired several pulses. Due to the close range, the damage inflicted was immense, and that shield dropped momentarily. Several dark circles littered the surface, courtesy of his railgun and laser, and the vessel smashed into another beside it, disabling that one's shield, too, and both crashed into the ground next to the rampaging herd of bioweapons.

"Thank you!" Bokerov shouted over the comm. "Finally, some action! Die, alien bitches!"

Jason glanced at his overhead map and saw that the forefront of the herd was only just reaching his position.

Those flyers continued to rain down. Another large ellipse appeared in front of him: the rectangular section that held the craft's turrets was pointed directly at him.

Before he could react, energy whips struck it courtesy of Iris, weakening the protective shield that enveloped the flyer; then Cheyanne appeared from behind and split the craft entirely in two, her swords easily penetrating the weakened shield. She was in the air, and began her spinning top maneuver, rotating around in a movement that was almost a blur, despite his Bullet Time. She closed with one of the flyers, and her swords bounced off its shields, but she was rotating so fast that incredible energy was imparted with each impact so that in only a few moments she'd disabled that shield, and instead her blades were digging into metal.

Aria had three tanks fire everything they had at a flyer, and then she unleashed her lightning bolt weapon at it, bringing it down.

Maeran sent her drones into another aircraft, and simply kept them in place around it so that the cutting triangular energy beam constantly enveloped the craft. The vessel tried to break free as its shield flashed incessantly under the strain; eventually the shield failed, and the energy beams cut the flyer in half.

Xin fired the energy beam from her eyes, following a flyer as it darted underneath the branches of a tree. Like Maeran, she kept the beam trained on the craft, and eventually the shield failed, and her beam ate through the fuselage.

That has to be draining on the battery, keeping that beam active like that.

Sophie meanwhile was concentrating on ravaging the herd that was running past her position, where she hid behind a tree. She revolved her micro machines around her, first left, then right, successively chopping into the Rhinoeyes that ran past. Sometimes she cut the weapons right off, or sheared off the knob of a head; sometimes, she merely bloodied the animals.

Drawn by the blood, the Rex Wolves fought close to her, and attacked any of the bioweapons that got past her barrage. They worked in pairs. Their modus operandi would involve one pinning a creature with its jaws, while the other chomped off the weapons. Bruiser almost took an energy blast to the mouth at one point as he ripped off a turret, but thankfully the weapon missed, hitting a nearby tree instead.

Lori was invisible, and she was firing plasma bolts at any flyer that got near Tara. Jason helped her, targeting the flyer with his laser, weakening the shield enough for Tara to stab through with her sword.

The battle proceeded in that manner for the next two minutes. Occasionally Jason or another War Forger stepped out too far from behind a tree where they had been hiding, and they were pummeled by a bioweapon. Usually the creature was too surprised by the impact to do anything while the stricken War Forger fired at point blank range. If the bioweapons didn't go down, they kept running.

Bokerov made short work of any survivors, his tanks and Cataphracts dispensing death while receiving little damage themselves. Those Cataphracts had attracted the attention of some of the flyers by then, and the bigger units had to deal with them, too. That wasn't difficult, given the array of huge energy and plasma beams some of those Cataphracts were equipped with.

And then, just like that, it was done. The enemy units ceased arriving. Around Jason and the others, the forest floor was littered with the wreckages of Tyrnari flyers, and the corpses of mutilated bioweapons.

"Well," Tara said. "That seemed a little too easy."

"That's because it was!" Cheyanne had used her wings to fly above the treetops overhead. "Those were just their scouts! The rest of the army is incoming."

Jason switched to her viewpoint and saw the sky littered with airships and flyers. There were literally hundreds of flyers approaching above the treetops. His counting algorithm reported one thousand three hundred twenty four. And one hundred fifty airships.

"There are definitely more than they started with," Jason said.

Mechs began to appear to the west, emerging through the foliage. Phasers, and a new type of unit: the size and shape was similar to that of a Modlenth mech, but the hull was covered in glowing plasma.

One of those new units pointed a hand at Aria, and a thick stream of plasma erupted from its hand, heading toward her; she barely swung her shield in place, and deflected the blow. The inside of her shield glowed red hot from impact, and as that attack continued, red became white.

"Can't hold it!" Aria dove behind a tree, moving out of the line of fire.

The plasma beam ceased. For now.

"Plasma Throwers!" Lori said.

"We figured that out," Maeran said.

Jason swung his energy weapon and railgun toward the new arrivals.

19

Before Jason could fire, plasma and energy bolts erupted from the trees to the northeast in a concerted bombardment that slammed into the newly arrived Imperial mechs. Most of the Phasers dematerialized, only to be slammed by more bolts when they returned to this reality.

"Hello, Earthers," Jhagan's voice came over the comm.

"Jhagan!" Jason said.

From the trees to the northwest, Modlenth mechs emerged. They continued to fire at the Imperials, forcing them back.

Jason realized Jhagan had been shadowing Jason's advance.

"Now would be a good time to run," Jhagan said. "We won't be able to hold them for long."

"You heard the man," Jason said. "Everyone, retreat to the south!"

Jason turned south. He glanced at his overhead map, and saw that his army was making an orderly retreat. He started to run, but then paused. "Why are you doing this?"

"We always pay back our favors," Jhagan said. "The queen sent me to ensure you made it safely to the rift. Go!"

Jason ran once more. He grabbed Shaggy by the collar, ensuring the animal went with him. Tara did the same with Bruiser and Lackey, while Lori handled Runt.

Jason recalled his Explorer, and hurried through the well-spaced trees, until the fighting was well behind him.

He sent the Explorer over the treetops and saw that the hundreds of Imperial flyers and airships had not pursued his retreating army; instead, they were moving eastward, and firing into the trees, no doubt at Jhagan's detachment, who were fleeing toward the main city. The Imperials would much rather destroy the Modlenth than a few "Earthers," as Jhagan had called them.

"We're just going to leave them?" Tara said. She must have been viewing the feed from the Explorer— he'd granted his core group access.

Jason hesitated. "What can we do? They're on their own now. We have a rift to catch."

"We should at least stay for a while, and see how they do," Xin said.

Three large Modlenth airships emerged from where they had been hiding underneath the trees, and opened fire at the smaller flyers in the vanguard, destroying them all. Then they accelerated away as they began to take fire from the more distant flyers.

"See, Jhagan will make it back to the city just fine," Jason said.

"It's not Jhagan I'm worried about," Xin said. "It's Risilan. If her city falls…"

"She's right," Aria said. "It's in our best interests to help them."

"How did I know you two would take the same side?" Tara said.

"Think about it," Aria said. "If Risilan loses, the Imperials will take over, and send their invasion force back to Earth to finish what they started."

"Sure, but just because Risilan wins, doesn't mean she won't also send an invasion force to Earth," Tara said. "For all her brave words about disavowing the empire, who knows what she'll do when we're gone. She might very well decide that whatever favor the empire grants her for more bioweapons will be worth the attempt to take over our planet. Especially if she plans on returning her planet to the way it was, and shutting down local bioweapon production here."

"No," Jason said. "She wouldn't betray us like that. I know she wouldn't. She rewards loyalty. She sent Jhagan to help us, didn't she?"

"We don't actually know whether she sent him," Tara said. "Or whether he came out of his own sense of obligation."

"I still think we should stay at least a little longer," Aria said. "To confirm that Risilan is going to win."

"I agree," Cheyanne said. "She might need the help of our army yet."

"She has the space navy at her command," Jerry said. "I think she'll be all right."

"Well if that's true," Cheyanne said. "How come this space navy of hers hasn't yet opened fire on the enemy units?"

"That's a good point," Jason said. "I'll try to ask Jhagan, while he's still in range." Jason switched to the common band, and directed his antennae toward the fleeing Modlenth. "Jhagan, why hasn't the space navy opened fire on the Imperials?"

"We can't," Jhagan said. "Prince Amadan planted what you would call a Trojan in the AI equivalents we have running the starships. He sent a rogue signal to those ships and disabled them all. We're trying to get them operational again, but it's doubtful they'll be ready anytime soon."

"Sounds like something Bokerov would do," Julian said.

"Thanks for the update," Jason told Jhagan.

Jason glanced at his overhead map. They still had quite a ways to go to reach the rift site. Whereas the city was a lot closer to the east.

"Damn," Jason said. "You know, there's a chance the city will fall before we reach the rift location. And if that happens..."

"Then there's no going home," Maegan said.

"We could increase our pace..." Sophie said. "We might still make it in time. We have to try. And if we do make it, even if the city falls, and the evil queen dies, it won't matter."

"What do you mean, it won't matter?" Aria said.

"We'll still have to deal with the Imperials when they return to Earth."

"Well I mean, we can plan an ambush," Sophie said. "We know where they're going to appear, so we can lay a shit ton of mines. And prepare energy turrets and defense platforms all over the area. Just get ready for a big-time ass kicking, if you know what I mean."

Jason shook his head. "I'm not sure we'd have time to set all that up. In fact, there might even be a detachment of Imperials waiting for us once we pass through, and we could end up fleeing the area." He paused. "No, this isn't right. We can't abandon the Modlenth, not yet. If we really want to defeat these Imperials, our best chance is right here, right now, while they're distracted by the Modlenth. We have to return to the city. Anyone who wants to continue to the rift may do so of course."

"I'll go with you, of course," Tara said.

"As will I," Sophie said. "Grudgingly."

"Anyone else want to go?" Jason asked.

All of the other War Forgers and their clones elected to remain with him.

"What about me, I don't get to return if I want?" Bokerov asked.

"Nope," Jason replied. "You're my slave. So." He studied his map. "It's going to be about a three hours return march. When we get there, we're just going to watch, for now."

"Just watch?" Aria said. "No intervening?"

"That's right," Jason said.

"But you just said, if we wanted to defeat the Imperials, our best chance was to strike while they were distracted by the Modlenth," Aria said.

"I did say that," Jason admitted. "But I don't want to intervene if the Modlenth are winning. If they're not, on the other hand, *then* I'll think about it. So, watching... that means hanging onto the Rex Wolves this time." He didn't want a repeat of the last incident, where the Rex Wolves ran headfirst into the Imperials and led them right to Jason's army.

He produced the collar from his storage compartment, and wrapped it around Shaggy's neck. Then he attached the leash. He handed the reins to Lori. "Take care of Shaggy for me."

"You got it," Lori said. She had Runt similarly leashed, while Tara handled Bruiser and Lackey.

Jason turned his army east. Well, slightly to the southeast, actually: he wanted to come at the city from the flank, and well away from the Imperials.

As expected, it took about three hours to return to the city. Jason was tempted to switch to VR for the journey, but decided he'd be better off personally watching the trees for signs of ambush now that the Imperials had returned. Repairs were essentially completed by that point, with only a few of the drones still making minor touch-ups to the Cataphracts, so Jason ordered all repair units to their respective storage compartments.

By then the siege was in full force, and Jason watched as the Imperial troops bombarded the city from the west side with everything they had. Almost all of the turrets that lined the base of the city's dome there had been destroyed, so that only a few returned fire. Also, there were no Modlenth flyers offering any defensive fire, nor any airships, while the Imperials still had thousands of the former, and hundreds of the latter. Jason didn't know where Jhagan's detachment had gone—hopefully they'd made it inside the city before the Imperials arrived.

"Well, they're doing fine, can we go now?" Tara asked.

"Doesn't look like they're doing all that fine to me," Xin commented.

"I'm with Tara on this one," Sophie said. "We should turn back. The Modlenth are doing just peachy. We've done enough for them."

As Jason watched, the last of the turrets on the western side was shot down. The large mass of enemy troops, both air and ground units, began to concentrate their fire at the base of the dome, toward the western half of the circular ring responsible for generating the protective field that enveloped the city. Plasma, lightning, and energy bolts and beams bombarded the metal surface, inflicting pockmarks and blast craters. Missiles smashed into the weakened surface, and the all too familiar black blobs flowed into the craters, expanding outward. The blobs hardened, and successive plasma impacts shattered the entire surface, breaking away large clumps.

In only a few minutes, holes began to appear in the ring, and yellow mist from the atmosphere flooded inside. Automated repair drones rushed to the damaged areas and attempted to stem the tide, but the enemy kept up their fire, and easily destroyed them.

As those gaps grew bigger, they affected the energy dome generated by the base so that long slivers appeared in the protective surface. Those slivers expanded with the gaps, forming large convex regions of unprotected space amid the dome. Soon those spaces outnumbered the intact areas so that slices of energy were the exception rather than the norm, and it looked almost like a few convex bars protected that side of the city, versus a solid wall everywhere else.

"I take back what I said a few minutes ago," Sophie said quietly.

Several of the Imperial airships landed in the no man's land between the forest and the wall, and they lowered big ramps to the ground. Before the ramps even touched down, huge herds of Rhinoeyes flowed out. They stampeded over the land so hard that Jason could feel the vibrations even from here. All of the creatures were wearing the weapon turret backpacks so that they acted like mini-gunships. Those turrets were firing at unseen targets past the broken wall as they ran toward the city.

"The Imperials are putting their new favorite bioweapon to use, I see," Jones commented. "I wonder if that's illegal, from an empire standpoint."

"I'm not sure the Imperials care, at this point," Jerry said.

The bioweapons flowed over the collapsed wall, followed by several Imperial mechs, both Phaser and Plasma Throwers. Flyers joined them, along with airships, firing down into the fray.

"It looks like it's getting fairly nasty in there," Maeran said.

"When are we going to join the attack?" Aria said.

"We'll wait until the Imperials commit more troops," Jason said. "Then we'll attack from behind."

"A pincer maneuver," Tara said. "I like it."

Jason waited, but only about half of the ground and air troops moved forward and into the city, while the rest remained behind, standing guard.

"Hmm," Xin said. "It looks like they're not going to commit much more than that."

She was right. A few minutes passed, and still those troops hadn't moved. They continued to fire into the city from their current positions.

"The original plan won't work then," Jason said. "Okay. We'll stay in the forest, and attack these guys instead. Bokerov, I want you to send your troops around to the west side of that detachment. Aria, return control of your tank platoon to him—he'll need them. When you're in place, Bokerov, we'll attack at the same time, you from the west, the War Forgers from the south. Your Cataphracts should be hidden by the tall trees... so you can use that to get close. But be careful not to let them detect your vibrations until I give the order to attack."

"I can do this," Bokerov said.

"It's still a pincer maneuver, of sorts," Aria said.

"That's right," Jason said.

"We're still vastly outnumbered, no matter how you look at it," Tara said. "We tried to fight this army before on Earth... you saw what happened then."

"That was on an open plain, and without an

outflanking strategy," Jason insisted. "Plus, they have half their numbers at the moment, with most in the city."

"True," Tara said. "But there are bound to be Imperial scouts out there, watching the detachment's rear. That outflanking strategy might not be as effective as you hope."

"I'm well aware that there could be enemy sentries present," Jason said. "Which is why I want Bokerov to give them as wide a berth as possible during his approach, while using scouts of his own."

"I'll take the utmost of care in my approach," Bokerov said.

"If you're detected," Jason said. "We'll just have to begin the attack earlier. Also, Bokerov, I want you to make sure you utilize your antennae in directional mode. Leave units behind at intervals to act as repeaters, forming a half-circle around the Imperials until you're in position. Direct all communications along that arcing line of repeaters to keep our transmissions hidden from them."

"I will do this," Bokerov said.

Jason ordered the War Forgers and their clones to move forward as well, staying inside the forest, until they were a kilometer to the south of the enemy line. Jason sent his Explorer forward, staying underneath the canopy of trees to avoid detection. He spotted one scout, and the team avoided it.

Jason and his group kept their antennae angled to the northwest, toward Bokerov's closest repeater unit. Even though the antennae were currently in directional mode, the comm systems also had an omnidirectional range of around fifty meters so that the local crew could still keep in contact with one other.

After Jason and the others were in place, they waited: it took Bokerov's detachment a little longer to move into position. The Russian had to avoid two enemy scouts in the forest along the way, and also cover more territory. Finally, his tanks and Cataphracts assumed their designated positions in the forest a kilometer west of the enemy line.

"We're in place," Bokerov said.

"Attack!" Jason said. "Originals and clones, that means you, too!"

Aria took the lead, and Jason followed behind her. Tara was at his right side, Lori his left. Both of the girls still hung onto the Rex Wolves by their leashes, and the mutants pulled wildly at the reins, literally tugging them forward as they tried to break free.

The other girls were spread out through the tall trees behind him, along with the other War Forger clones.

They were three hundred meters away when Aria's shield began to glow red at different spots along the inside.

"We're taking fire!" Aria said.

20

"Take cover behind the trees!" Jason said.

Jason dodged behind the closest trunk with Aria. It was thick enough to hold them both.

Tara and Lori had taken cover behind other trees nearby, and they were still reining in the Rex Wolves, who were barking wildly.

Aria swiveled her lightning weapon past the left edge of the trunk, while Jason did the same on the opposite side with his energy weapon. He switched his point of view to the weapon scope, and surveyed the trees. He spotted Phaser and Plasma Thrower mechs taking cover behind different trunks. He aimed at a Phaser's sword that was exposed, and fired. The Phaser didn't wink out—apparently it hadn't detected the attack in time—and the tip of the weapon melted before the owner pulled it out of view entirely.

Jason tried targeting the trunk next; he wondered

how deep his energy bolt would penetrate. He fired, and carved a blast hole into the wood, while the imparted shockwave launched shards of wood in every direction. However, the penetration wasn't as deep as he'd hoped. He might be able to shoot right through the edge of it after five more shots. Targeting the center would take a lot more. Sturdy trees.

A plasma bolt from another attacker struck his forearm, narrowly missing his energy weapon, and he pulled back behind cover.

Bolts began to shred the branches above as enemy fire rained down from flyers that had positioned overhead.

Aria immediately tilted her shield upward to protect herself and Jason.

Cheyanne darted skyward, and began her spinning top routine. Sophie activated her jumpjets and unleashed her micro machines at other flyers to draw their fire.

Cheyanne only managed to take down two of the shielded units before one of her wings was shot off. Sophie caught her, and lowered her safely to the ground behind a tree.

Jason aimed skyward, and unleashed several blows in rapid succession, breaking through the shield, and then striking the fuselage of the flyer underneath. Xin fired at the same target, and cut through the craft, sending it falling in multiple pieces.

One of the enemy missiles struck the tree beside Jason. Black goo began to flow over the surface. Jason and Aria stepped backward, away from the tree. Another bolt struck it from the other side, and the entire section coated by that goo shattered; the tree pitched precariously to the right and began to topple.

"Cover us!" Jason and Aria retreated into the open and dashed behind another tree for cover.

Jason glanced at his overhead map. Bokerov's troops had vanished entirely from the display. "What the—"

Jason dispatched his Explorer to the west. The scout darted through the trees, while Jason continued attacking the enemy, sometimes aiming at the ground troops hidden behind the trees ahead, at other times firing between the boughs overhead at the latest flyers.

"Alien bombers!" Maeran said.

Jason accelerated his time sense, and glanced through the boughs overhead. He spotted the falling bombs that Maeran had highlighted.

"All right, reposition!" Jason said. He circled the new location, three hundred meters to the northwest. He hoped it was far enough.

Jason returned his time sense to something more manageable, and then dashed from the trees with Aria at his side. She had her shield in place between him and the attacks. While on the run, they fired around the shield, at the Imperials hidden behind the trees across from them. The rest of the War Forgers and their clones followed just behind, and were also firing.

Jason reached the target waypoint and dove behind a tree. The other War Forgers took cover just as a massive shockwave of energy dissolved the area behind them. In place of the forest there, and the ground where the trees had grown, only a crater remained—its walls a perfectly smooth half sphere.

Jason glanced at his status display. All of the War Forgers had survived, and successfully repositioned. The Imperial troops had followed their progress, and continued firing from the trees ahead. Flyers moved into the area cleared by the bomb, and fired not just from above, but from that clearing, too, now.

"It was only one bomber," Xin announced. "I got it, I think."

"Good job," Jason said.

He concentrated his fire on the flyers that were in the open above the new crater. He took one down by combining his attack with Aria.

After it crashed, he felt the ground rumbling around him.

"The Imperials have dispatched a reserve herd of bioweapons!" Jones said. "The Imperials are trying to flush us out!"

Rhinoeyes dashed by on either side of the tree where Aria and Jason resided. Jason fired intermittently at them, cutting thick gashes into their sides as they drove past. Some of the bioweapons attempted to pull up short to engage him, but others plowed into them from behind.

"Not very effective in closed quarters, are they?" Aria said.

Across from him, Cheyanne sliced out with her swords, cutting through any of the bioweapons that got close.

Tara and Lori held onto the Rex Wolves, keeping them hidden behind the trees; the mutants bit into the necks of passing Rhinoeyes.

While that was taking place, the Explorer finally approached Bokerov's position, and Jason focused his attention on the video feed the drone transmitted.

The tanks and Cataphracts under the Russian's control were idling.

No wonder this is so damn hard.

"Bokerov, attack!" Jason ordered.

A laugh came over the comm channel used by the Explorer.

"You're an idiot," Bokerov said over that same channel. "I broke free of your Containment Code hours ago. I'm not your slave anymore, Shit Eater. You thought you'd use me to outflank the Tyrnari? Now the Tyrnari and I are going to outflank *you*."

Turrets on nearby tanks swiveled toward the Explorer. Jason quickly recalled it, and bolts raked the air behind the scout.

Jason remembered the earlier strange transmission Bokerov had made. He slowed down his time sense.

"Lori, I've lost Bokerov," Jason said. "I think because of the transmission Bokerov made earlier."

"It's my fault," Lori said. "I obviously made a mistake somewhere in the Containment Code I injected. My guess is he used a zero day vulnerability in your comm line, one that hasn't been patched since his time, and used it to obtain your comm header signature. With that, he could mimic any request from you, including a command to lift the Containment Code.

That's my working theory, anyway: I wasn't able to access his backup activity log to confirm any of that."

"Should we combine?" Jones said.

"Not yet," Jason said. "With both Bokerov and the Imperials out there firing at us, combining would be a disaster. We stay in cover for now. Lori, do what you can to re-enable that Containment Code."

"I think I might have a way," Lori said. "But I'll have to get closer."

"You could have used whatever it is you're planning on him earlier," Sophie said. "When he was in range."

"Yes, but I didn't know he'd broken free of the Code," Lori said.

"Why do you have to get close?" Jason asked Lori.

"He's stopped broadcasting directionally," Lori replied. "I'm going to have to approach to within fifty meters of one of his units to tap into his localized omni-directional adhoc network."

"I'll escort you," Jason said. "Aria, you're with me! The rest of you, cover us!"

"The Rhinoeyes the enemy released will probably do a good job of that!" Iris said. "Covering you, I mean!"

Lori tossed the leashes of Runt and Shaggy to Sophie, who was hiding behind the same tree as her. "Hang onto them for me!"

Sophie's avatar displayed an expression of disgust, but she held on to the reins.

The Rhinoeyes had stopped rushing past by then; most had turned back, and now they alternately fired and rushed the different positions where the War

Forgers were taking cover. Meanwhile, the flyers overhead continued their assault.

Jason emerged from the tree where he had taken cover, and Aria joined him. She kept her shield in place, protecting him and her own mech from incoming fire from the Imperials on the right. Lori also moved west, but she was invisible, and didn't have to worry about attracting fire, at least for now.

Jason's left side was exposed to the Rhinoeyes, and he did his best to injure the bioweapons as he ran; he targeted that single big eye to blind them.

The other War Forgers and their clones similarly attacked those bioweapons, keeping them well distracted, allowing the trio to break free of the Rhinoeyes.

Soon, Jason, Lori and Aria had left the main fighting behind, and were stealthily making their way toward Bokerov's army. Well, as stealthily as big machines like themselves could move, at least. The noise of the distant battle easily covered that of their servomotors.

They were about two hundred meters from the outskirts of Bokerov's army, or at least the last known position as reported by the Explorer, when plasma bolts unleashed from the undergrowth ahead.

Aria and Jason dodged behind a tree, pinned down. They aimed past, returning fire, and ducked again as plasma bolts came back at them.

"Lori, you'll have to continue on your own until you're in range," Jason said.

"Will do," Lori said.

She approached on her own, remaining invisible. She kept her directional antenna pointed away from Bokerov, so as not to give away her position, while still staying in contact with Jason.

"Okay, I'm within fifty meters of one of his tanks," Lori said.

A timebase request had accompanied the message, and he'd automatically switched to his maximum time sense, to match Lori's own timebase. Everything froze around him.

"I've amped up my time sense, because he'll be able to read me, now," Lori said. "I'm working on my idea. But first I'll have to find a working backdoor."

"You mean we came all this way, and you don't even have a backdoor yet?" Jason said. He couldn't help the exasperation in his tone.

"Oh, hush," Lori said. "I'll find a way. It just might take some time. I have a bunch of ideas I want to try, using what I learned in my last attempts. I was almost through earlier, but then got distracted by the alien army, and well, you know, I never got the chance…"

Long moments passed. At least ten minutes at his current time sense, though only a few seconds had passed in the real world.

Jason was beginning to get antsy. "Well, what's going on?"

"Almost got it," Lori said.

More moments passed. Jason wasn't sure how much longer he could hold out. Time was still frozen around him; he was hidden behind the tree trunk, so he couldn't even see any of Bokerov's troops, let alone Lori.

But he knew their last known positions, as recorded on his overhead map. It was possible there was a shell speeding his way at that very moment. He'd know soon enough, he supposed. Time wasn't moving *that* slowly... any shells would still impact, and he'd see the fragments break away from the tree beside him.

"Okay," Lori finally said. "One of the backdoors was accessible—he hadn't patched it properly, and I was able to brute force my way inside. Everything was fairly locked down when I got inside... he activated some sort of sandbox environment in an attempt to contain me, but I broke free by creating a custom VR partition, using some hooks in his codebase I left last time... hooks Bokerov had overlooked, and hadn't yet cleaned up."

"So he's in our control?" Jason asked.

"Not yet," Lori said. "I'll need your help to install the final piece. You'll have to join me in VR. And I have to warn you though, Bokerov will have complete control over your avatar once you're inside. He may do unpleasant things to you."

"That's fine," Jason said. "Tell me what to do."

And she did.

"I'm coming, too," Aria said.

"You'll see a request to join my VR," Lori said. "When you accept, you'll actually be joining Bokerov's custom VR partition, to which I've created a virtual tether."

"That's fine, whatever we need to do to break Bokerov..." Jason said.

Assuming Bokerov didn't break Jason and the others

first.

Jason received a request to log into Lori's custom VR, and he accepted.

21

Jason resided on a wide steppe. He was on a horse, bareback. The grass reached to its knees.

He was dressed in a loincloth made of animal hide. His bare skin was covered in grime, and he carried a thick wooden club with spikes on the tip. His hair was long, greasy, as was his beard.

Aria was on horseback beside him. She was dressed just as simply, in a bikini made of tanned skins. Her hair was twined into a long ponytail that reached to the middle of her back. Her pale skin was covered in grime, like Jason's. There was no sign of the fangs she sometimes wore, but she did hold a long morning star with a spiked head attached to the tip of the shaft by a chain.

"Where's Lori?" Aria said.

"I don't know," Jason said. "But obviously Bokerov is already in control. I didn't choose these clothes for my avatar. How about you?"

"Not my choice, either," Aria said.

Jason tried to pull up his HUD, but the interface refused to appear.

"Do you have access to your HUD?" Jason asked.

"Nope," Aria replied.

Movement drew Jason's eye to another horse in the distance. A man resided in the saddle. He wore chain-mail armor, with a coif that wrapped his head but left the face bare, and he carried a longsword polished to a sheen.

"Shit Eater!" the man shouted.

"Bokerov," Jason said softly.

"Finally you get to see me," Bokerov said. "What an honor this is for you, is it not? You should have accepted my invitation to join my VR earlier. We could have gotten this over with hours ago! Oh well, now's as good a time as any. I'm a big believer in fair fights. Unlike you, who enslaved me without even giving me a chance to defend myself."

"You had your chance in the real world," Jason said.

"But not the virtual, where it counted," Bokerov said.

"Well nothing in this virtual environment is fair," Jason said. "Everything here will be tipped to your favor."

"I don't think so," Bokerov said. "After all, there are two of you, and only one of me. It's certainly a fair fight. Though more tipped, as you say, in your favor than mine."

Bokerov spurred his horse to a gallop. He raised his sword as he raced toward Aria and Jason.

"Well," Jason said. "I guess we fight, then."

He had practiced horseback riding a few times in his own VR, so he knew how to ride. Apparently Aria did as well, because when he spurred the animal forward she joined him.

Jason raised his club, and Aria her morning star.

Bokerov meanwhile bent his arm and held his sword behind his head, in a pose that seemed to be in preparation for stabbing.

As they passed, the sword enlarged by an alarming degree. The weapon moved in a blur, and before Jason could react, his body was slit in half.

The upper part of his torso dropped to the grass, his guts oozing out underneath him. Aria's head landed beside him.

"Well, that was really fair," Aria commented.

The virtual environment reset, and Jason was on horseback beside Aria once more, while Bokerov waited across the field. This time, the Russian was on foot.

"Let's do this again, shall we?" Bokerov shouted. "A hundred times. A thousand. Shit, I can do this to the end of time. I'll devote a background process to this VR partition, and let it run indefinitely. I'll kill you a billion times. Meanwhile, I'll slaughter the rest of your Shit Eaters, and then replay their deaths for you for all eternity."

Bokerov began running at them.

"Let's not stick around, huh?" Jason told Aria.

"I'm for that…" Aria said.

They both turned their horses around, and then proceeded away at a gallop.

"Oh no you don't," Bokerov said. It sounded like the Russian was just behind them.

Jason was about to turn around when Bokerov appeared in front of him. His sword had become a long staff with blades on either end, and he sliced the weapon underneath the legs of the two horses, severing the forelimbs of both virtual animals at the same time.

Two quick stabs, and he put Jason and Aria out of their misery.

The VR environment reset once more.

This time Jason was standing in the desert with a long dagger in hand. Beside him was a tree. Aria was tied to it with her arms spread-eagled. They both still wore the flimsy garments.

"Let's try something different," Bokerov said.

"Bored of killing us already?" Aria commented.

Bokerov ran a hand up Aria's bare thigh. "Oh yes, there are so many more ways to inflict lasting psychological damage. All of them pleasurable for me."

Jason struck at Bokerov with the sword, but he froze in place.

Bokerov raised an admonishing finger. "Uh, uh, uh. This time, you're going to kill her, not me. And slowly."

"No, I won't," Jason said.

"Yes, you will," Bokerov said.

Jason's body turned of its own accord. He fought the force that was in control of him, and managed to halt his rotation, but felt an incredible pain inside of him at the same time; that pain quickly became overwhelming, and he gave in, if only so the pain would subside.

"Good," Bokerov said. "Now cut off her clothes."

Jason did so, wanting to avoid that pain.

"Now, remove the skin of her right leg," Bokerov said.

Jason refused.

The pain became overwhelming inside of him. It felt like he was tied at the stake, with a raging fire burning all around him, consuming his flesh, blackening it, charring it.

His hand shook violently from the sheer force of will required to restrain the blade.

"No," Jason said.

"Yes," Bokerov said. "You will do it, or the pain will consume your consciousness. Break you utterly."

"Then let it break me," Jason said.

He felt to his knees, screaming.

"Just cut open my leg!" Aria shouted.

At last Jason ceded, and he stabbed the dagger deep into her calf. She flinched, and screamed.

"There, that wasn't so hard, was it?" Bokerov said.

Jason suddenly withdrew the blade and stabbed it home, right through Bokerov's chain mail.

Bokerov looked down at his impaled chest in confusion. "How?"

Jason twisted the dagger, and Bokerov flinched in pain.

"Lori gave me a few routines she thought I might need against you," Jason said.

Jason was about to twist the blade again when he froze once more.

"Ah yes, I see the backdoors," Bokerov said. "I've already patched them."

Jason's arm moved backward, withdrawing the blade of its own accord. He couldn't even resist it at all this time. There was no pain, no nothing.

"Maybe we'll do this the easy way," Bokerov said. "I'll take control of your body, and you'll simply watch."

Jason flicked the blade toward Aria once more. There was fear in her eyes, and yet also defiance.

"I'm sorry," Jason said.

"Maybe we won't skin her just yet," Bokerov said. "Maybe we'll have some fun with her first. You can watch as I ravage her. Would you like that?"

"You're sick," Aria said.

"I sometimes forget how twisted you are, Bokerov," Jason said. "I have to thank you for reminding me why I can never let you go. Why you must always be a slave."

"Except I'm not anymore," Bokerov said, grinning. "Now then, where were we?"

Bokerov took a step toward Aria, and then she abruptly stiffened. "No!"

The environment faded out.

Jason and Aria stood on the edge of some sort of cliff. Beside them, was a mountain temple; monks in orange robes sat upon the steps, and between the pillars, locked in prayer.

Bokerov's voice carried from somewhere ahead.

"This is my most sacred place!" Bokerov shouted. "How dare you intrude!"

The ledge continued past a bend in the mountain wall. Bokerov's voice seemed to come from there.

Jason rounded the bend and then he saw Lori, dressed in brilliant silver plate mail. She wasn't wearing a helmet: her long blond hair flowed down to her shoulders. She carried a longsword, and exchanged blows with Bokerov. Both of their swords moved in a blur: it was almost transfixing to watch.

"Jason!" Lori said, not breaking her gaze from Bokerov. "Your distraction worked! Mostly!"

"What do you mean *mostly?*" Jason said as he came running up beside her. "Do you have control, or not?"

"I've trapped him in this current form!" Lori said. "He can't transform his weapons, or materialize more. Nor can he control us!"

"You bitch!" Bokerov said. His movements increased, and he steadily beat her back, forcing her on the defensive.

There were two swords stabbed into the dirt nearby, point first. Jason and Aria grabbed one each.

"Do you have any sword experience?" Jason asked Aria.

"Nope," Aria said. "I'm having my Accomp take over as we speak."

"Z, you here?" Jason asked.

"I am," Z replied.

"Tell me you have some swordplay routines in your database," Jason said.

"I do," Z said. "You want me to overlay some Training AIs over your vision?"

"Don't think there's time," Jason said. "But if you wouldn't mind taking over…"

Z did so, and immediately Jason's body moved

forward to join the fray. His sword moved in a blur besides Lori. Aria joined in a moment later. The three of them managed to put Bokerov on the defensive, and pushed him backward, toward the precipitous drop that awaited beyond the ledge.

"We can't let him fall!" Lori said as Bokerov came close.

At that, Bokerov, in between parries, cocked his head. And then he leaped off.

"No!" Lori said. She vaulted off the ledge after him.

Jason tried to catch her, but missed, and fell, too.

Bokerov hit a rocky outcrop, and bounced off slightly; Lori and Jason smashed into it as well. They all bounced off the rocky wall several times on the way down. Wasn't pleasant.

Finally, broken and bloodied, Jason hit the ground. Every virtual bone was broken in his body. Lori seemed in just as bad a condition, as did Bokerov.

Incredibly, Lori pulled herself upright on one arm. She coughed blood, but slowly dragged herself toward Bokerov's motionless body.

"You bitch," Bokerov said. "You'll pay for this." Blood trickled down his lips.

He tried to raise his sword when Lori reached him, but a bone abruptly protruded from his wrist, thanks to the weight of the weapon, and he dropped it.

Lori pulled herself on top of him.

"What, you're going to fuck me, like this?" Bokerov said between bloody teeth. He grinned.

"Oh, I'm going to fuck you all right," Lori said.

Her avatar descended into Bokerov's, until in

moments, she completely overlaid his, and was no longer visible.

"Where did she go?" Bokerov said.

He twitched suddenly, and then began spasming.

"That's right," Jason said. "Enjoy having your insides rearranged."

"Nyet!" Bokerov screamed.

"Too late," Lori said, stepping out of his avatar.

A HUD appeared. Jason immediately reset his avatar, and then stood.

Aria appeared next to Lori. She gazed down at the broken and sobbing body. "You did it, I assume?"

Lori nodded. She turned toward Jason. "His army is yours once more."

"Bokerov, engage the enemy with your Cataphracts and tanks, as per the original plan," Jason ordered

Still lying down, Bokerov nodded in defeated. "Done."

He glanced Lori. "You've locked down his code for good this time?"

"I think so," Lori said. "I've put in so many back-doors and hooks, I'll know right away if he ever tries to break free. And I can punish him for the attempts. I've also nested the Containment Code, wrapping one layer of control above the next, so that if he does somehow manage to defeat one layer, I'll instantly be notified, and can create more layers while punishing him in the process. There are more nested layers of Containment Code than a Russian matryoshka doll."

"Why do you have to refer to my current state in that manner?" Bokerov whined. "A Russian doll is supposed to be a toy for children to play with. A happy toy."

"I thought you'd appreciate the metaphor," Lori told him. "Because for me, you essentially are a toy. We're not going to forget how you treated us and our clones in here. Not ever."

"All right," Jason said. "Let's not overdo the gloating. Let's get back to our reality. We have a fight to win."

22

J ason returned to reality, and lowered his time sense to something more manageable, and the world was no longer frozen around him. He tentatively peered around the edge of the tree, and was relieved to see Bokerov's troops obediently moving to the east, toward the Imperials, rather than opening fire on his current position.

Jason also confirmed that Bokerov's units appeared on the overhead map once again.

"Bokerov is back on our side," Jason transmitted to the War Forgers and their clones.

"About time," Jerry said.

"How are we doing on the Imperial bioweapons?" Jason asked.

"We've almost eliminated all of them," Jerry replied. "Problem is, the enemy mechs are still keeping us pinned, and the flyers still harass us from above. Plus they've positioned a few of their airships overhead, and have been raining down hell."

"Combine as soon as Bokerov begins the attack," Jason said. "We'll win this yet. Are you able to tell how the battle inside the city is going?"

"No," Jerry said. "We're just going to have to hope that Risilan can hold off the prince's detachment until we can clean up out here."

Jason, Aria and Lori rushed back toward the other Originals. Tara, Sophie and Xin met them halfway; Maeran, Iris and Cheyanne were also with the three of them, along with the Rex Wolves. Iris and Cheyanne were hanging onto the leashes of the dogs, for now.

"You should have stayed with the clones," Jason accosted Maeran, Iris and Cheyanne.

"No," Maeran said. "You're our battle leader. We belong with you."

By then, according to the map, Bokerov's units had reached the west side of the Imperials, and had begun to bombard the aliens, so Jason initiated the combine. The other War Forgers were doing likewise, judging from the way their dots moved together on the overhead map.

Jason flashed into his virtual reality, and held hands with the waiting girls.

They joined minds, and he knew all their deepest, darkest secrets, and also felt their hopes and dreams, and the fears they had about the coming battle. He had slept with each of them at least once by that point. They had truly become his battle harem. He loved them all, and they would know that now, in this fleeting moment while they were combined. And he realized that they all loved him too, in return, despite the masks they might wear when separated.

"We'll do well," Jason said. "I know we will."

"I hope you're right," Xin said.

Jason returned to the real world, and waited while the different mechs mounted one another, forming the final, joined body.

When it was done, he sat his final form upright, and then clambered to his feet, towering nearly to the top of the canopy formed by the trees. He had to bow his head slightly to fit beneath the branches.

On the ground beside him, Cheyanne, Maeran, Iris, and the dogs reached to his hips.

"It's time to help the Modlenth," Jason said.

He turned to the northeast, and hurried to join the front lines of the attack from that direction.

When Jason could make out the Imperial mechs in the foliage ahead, and the flyers darting underneath the trees to fire at other combined Cataphracts, Iris and Cheyanne unleashed the dogs. The Rex Wolves raced into the fray, ripping and tearing.

Jason fired the plasma beam from his hip, and tore a swath through several Plasma Throwers. He also hit a few Phasers, who faded out before the impact. He followed up with quick railgun bursts from his shoulder to eliminate the Phasers when they reappeared.

A missile came in from above the trees, and Jason raised his shield. It impacted: black liquid coated a small portion along the edge of the shield, solidifying a moment later. He rubbed the glob with his finger, breaking away the affected portion—might as well rid himself of the damaged section now, since it would crumble as soon as an enemy struck it.

He approached the area where the alien bomber had carved a clearing in the trees. Most of the Cataphracts were occupied there.

Jason fired the energy cannon on his shoulder, targeting the different flyers. Airships were also there, hovering above the crater, and one of them unleashed a barrage his way; he was forced to bring his shield in front of him.

He reached John at the edge of the crater, who was also shielding himself. Jerry was doing the same beside him.

"Use your shields!" Jason said. "Bowl them over!"

Jason, John, and Jerry interlocked their shields, and stepped into the smooth blast crater. The dirt shifted under their weight, creating small steps in the concave surface.

Flyers attacked from behind, and Jason activated his body-wide energy shield for protection, as did John and Jerry.

Jason and the others batted aside the smaller flyers in front of them with their shields; usually the craft recovered, but some crashed into nearby trees, or the ground. When they reached the airships that were hovering just inside the crater at torso height, they promptly shoved their shields into the larger craft, and forced them to tip over.

The exposed vessels didn't crash, so Jason moved his shield out of the way and sliced through one of them.

John and Jerry did the same with the other airships in front of them.

Some of the bulky airships behind them tried to take flight, but the Cataphracts of Jones and Julian intercepted them from behind and swung their swords into the ships, taking them down. When they crashed, sometimes the units spilled mechs, other times bioweapons. Sometimes they were empty.

Either way, the dogs, along with Cheyenne, Maeran, and Iris, were there to intercept the smaller opponents.

When the crater was clear, Jason turned around. So far none of the other mechs had attacked. They were occupied defending against Bokerov, at least that was what the map reported. The sky was still full of flyers that were constantly incoming to assault Jason and his team, however.

Jason's energy shield was still active, protecting him from those assaults, but it ran out of power and failed soon after.

"Well, we can't teleport anymore, nor turn invisible," Aria said. "You spent all the power we had for those operations on the force field. And we can fire limited energy, plasma and lightning bolts."

"That's fine," Jason said. "We still have our sword, and ballistic shield."

Jason lifted the shield into place, and then rushed the flyers. He swept his sword in an arcing motion, and cut through four of the flyers at once. Their shields had been weakened from the previous strikes the War Forgers had made while separated, and probably from Bokerov's attacks.

With those flyers clear, he returned to the forest. Several of the trees here had fallen in the attack. Those that remained were mostly stripped of their leaves, allowing Jason to sight the different flyers and airships that remained above them.

He cut through those branches with his sword, making room to attack the flyers beyond. The Imperial airships and flyers got smart then, and pulled to a greater height. That only further exposed them to Bokerov's army, and the Cataphracts and tanks from the west side lit into them.

Jason held his shield in place, waiting for his energy cannon to recharge.

"Give us a boost," Cheyanne said.

Jason saw Cheyanne, Maeran and Iris waiting on the ground beside him. He scooped up each of them in turn, and threw them at the different airships. Cheyanne couldn't fly on her own—her wings were still damaged from a previous attack, and she hadn't yet repaired them.

Cheyenne landed on one of the big airships—its shield was down, thanks to previous attacks. She stabbed it with her swords, cutting a huge gash into its side, and sending it keeling off course. She leaped away before incoming fire could strike her, and repeated the process on another airship.

Iris used her whips to cut off pieces of the airships in turn, and dig deep gashes, while at the same time dodging blows coming at her. It usually took her ten to twenty seconds to damage an airship enough to crash it. It took Maeran about the same amount of time with her three energy drones. Their attacks ended when they attempted to leap onto airships that were still shielded, and they bounced away, landing on the forest floor, where they had to deal with the Phasers and Plasma Throwers.

Thanks to the sunlight streaming down, Jason had enough power to fire his energy cannon again, and he did so, tearing into the shielded vessel. John and Jerry fired at the same time, eliminating the shield, and allowing Jones and Julian to finish it off with their own cannons. The remaining airships decided to retreat, leaving only the flyers, which were still exposed to Bokerov's tanks and Cataphracts.

Jason dismissed those flyers for now, and moved deeper into the trees to concentrate on the Imperial mechs.

Flashes continually went off below hip height as Bokerov's tanks inflicted plasma and energy bolt damage against the Phasers and Plasma Throwers around him. Some of Bokerov's Cataphracts also continued to fire energy beams and bolts at the flyers, keeping them occupied.

The Octopus Cataphract was fighting nearby, and reared on its tentacles to fire the energy cannon from its maw. The targeted flyer accelerated out of the way, and the Octopus rotated the beam, trying to hit it, and instead struck Jason's Cataphract.

Jason swiveled his body aside, bringing his shield to bear, intercepting the blow. A big chunk was eaten out of his left side.

"Watch it!" Jason said.

"Sorry," Bokerov said.

Jason continued to attack the mechs with the other combined Cataphracts at his side.

"Maybe we should have never evacuated the plains of Earth in the first place," Sophie said. "We might have been able to take these bastards after all."

"I guess we'll never know now," Jerry said.

"You're forgetting that half the army is still inside the city," Jason said.

He was struck by a black blob missile in the hip, and in the shoulder, and portions of his combined body dissolved, but the AI cores of the respective mechs remained unharmed.

Jason sought out the source of those missiles, and hewed down the mechs responsible. One of them was a Phaser, and it winked out of existence, so Jason simply swung his sword in a pendulum fashion, timing the rebound with the Phaser's reappearance.

When he had enough power, he used his tail to fire thick plasma bolts at the enemy. He often targeted flyers with it, preferring to utilize his sword and shield for any mechs or bioweapons that presented themselves. He'd alternately hack with his sword, splitting a mech apart, and then bash with his shield, smashing a mech into a tree. If the unit survived the impact, he'd follow up with an energy attack if he had the power, and a sword stab if he did not.

Meanwhile, the Rex Wolves fought beside him, destroying enemy mechs like the best of them.

The debris piled up around Jason and the Cataphract clones until finally there were no more foes to take down. It actually came as a surprise. He destroyed his latest foe, and was looking around, searching for the next mech to target, but none presented themselves.

He glanced skyward. Bokerov had taken out the remaining flyers. Either that, or they had fled, perhaps to join their brethren in the city.

"We did it," Lori said.

"Not yet," Jason said. He turned toward the city and then marched through the trees. "Bokerov, War Forgers, line up under the eaves of the forest. Or what remains of it."

He maneuvered to the forest edge to overlook the city. He was expecting to see flashes, or explosions, or other signs of fighting, but the city was completely quiet. The western wall was still smashed to the ground in several places, and the energy dome mostly inactive on that side. From where he stood, he could see several neighborhoods reduced to rubble, with the triangular buildings toppled and smashed on the streets. There were also the wreckages of mechs from both sides, Imperial and Modlenth, intermixed with flyers and airships. It reminded Jason of the carnage at the battle site he'd just left behind.

"Forward, War Forgers!" Jason said. "Bokerov, stay where you are. Cover us."

"Okay," Bokerov said. "I'm your bitch."

"You certainly are," Jason said.

Jason and the others approached the smoking ruins of the city wall.

Inside, on the far side of the smashed buildings, he

spotted mechs hiding in the rubble. He thought they were Modlenth. When they didn't fire, he knew that he had guessed right.

Three Modlenth mechs emerged from cover, and made their way over the debris. They approached the ruined wall. One of them had a topknot on its head.

"We did it, with your help," Risilan said. "When you distracted the attackers outside the city walls, we were able to turn the tide. When the prince went down, the remaining mechs tried to flee. We slaughtered them."

"Kind of you," Sophie said.

"Merciful is a more accurate word," Risilan said.

"Evil bitch," Sophie muttered on a private line meant for the War Forgers only.

"She was only doing what she has to do to secure her throne," Aria said. "What we would do, if our homeland was threatened."

"Defend her all you want," Sophie said. "That doesn't change the fact that she's a murderer."

"Are we any better?" Iris said. "We just slaughtered an entire army. There were living Tyrnari piloting those flyers and mechs."

Sophie didn't have anything to say to that. None of them did.

One of the Modlenth mechs stepped away from the others, and held up the severed body sac of what could only be one of the Imperials.

"The prince," Risilan said. The mech, obviously hers, tossed the body sac into the air, and it landed on the ground outside the wall, deflating.

A strange, distorted screeching went up from the mechs behind her.

"Is that supposed to be a cheer?" Cheyanne said.

"Probably," Jason said.

"It's time to begin the long repairs," Risilan said. "My planet is safe, for now. Come with me, Jason. We have much to discuss."

"What's to discuss, other than our return home?" Jason said.

"As I said, much," Risilan told him.

23

J ason sat on the hardwood floor of the family room of his VR home and gazed out the floor-to-ceiling window toward the lake beyond.

Risilan shifted beside him where she lounged, and he turned his attention to her. The tiara and its teardrop brooch rested on her long, curly red hair. As usual, her cheeks were rosy, and her eye makeup smoky. The red and gold gown was spread out on the floor around her. Her expression seemed almost impatient.

Jason smiled slightly at the thought, and then gazed once more out at the lake.

"You know, I modeled all of this after a real location," Jason said. "A quaint little lake in the mountains. It was more commercialized than this, of course, with a chalet, and chairlifts for skiers. And the summer days were never this warm. But I made it my own." His smile became sad. "I can never go there in real life. Not now. At least, not in my present form."

"Why?" Risilan said.

"Because it's on the wrong side of the planet," Jason said. "The western hemisphere, where the rest of humanity lives. If I go there, the humans and their machines will hunt me and my girls down. I'm stuck in the irradiated zone. The closest I'll ever get to that lake is right here. And maybe that's for the best."

"Then why go back?" Risilan said. "If humanity hates you so much?"

"Because it's my home," Jason said. "And not all of humanity hates me. Only some of their governments. Well, they don't really hate me so much as fear me. They want to control me, I would assume. They did make me, after all, and I'm just their property, as far as they're concerned."

"To be one's property, is no different than slavery, is it not?" Risilan said.

"Yes," Jason said. "But they don't view it that way. Our laws are slightly outdated, and don't recognize Mind Refurbs as real people. Just soulless copies. That's gotta change. I don't know how, or when, but it has to. And someday, I'm hopeful the human governments will be able to come to some sort of arrangement with me, allowing android versions of myself and the girls to coexist in their cities."

"I see," Risilan said.

"No you don't," Jason said.

"No," Risilan admitted. "Your ways are alien to us."

"Not so alien, I'm sure," Jason said. "Your species once had slaves, didn't it?"

"At one point, yes," Risilan said. "But most

intergalactic races are guilty of the charge. It is one of the unfortunate aspects that come with the development of civilization. Someone has to build the infrastructure these civilizations use, until automatons are developed."

Jason stared into her eyes. He could lose himself in those deep, blue orbs.

It's all fake, he reminded himself. *She looks like a tentacled sac in real life.*

Still, it was pleasant to pretend.

"So why did you ask me here?" Jason said.

She swallowed, betraying the first sign of nervousness he had ever seen from her. She folded her hands, and looked down at them. "Well, I was thinking. I could use someone like you. Loyalty, a fierce spirit, and the ability to defend are rare traits these days, especially in the same individual. I was wondering if you'd be interested in joining my royal guard."

"Not interested," Jason said flatly. "I don't think I could stand to serve anyone else. Not after the leadership role I've filled since having my consciousness embedded in this body."

"What if I offered you the position of king, as my mate?" she pressed.

Jason stared at her, dumbfounded. Her expression was unreadable. Then finally: "You would do this?"

"I would," Risilan said.

Jason couldn't hide his skepticism. "But we can't even mate."

"Not physically," Risilan agreed. She gestured to the VR around her. "But here we can."

"Would you even feel pleasure?" Jason said.

"I've remapped the sexual organs of this virtual body to match the appropriate organs on my own body," Risilan said. "When stimulated, those virtual organs will activate the associated centers of my tri-brain. So yes, I will feel pleasure."

Jason still couldn't believe she wanted this. He shook his head in confusion.

"Why me?" Jason said. "You barely know me."

"Oh, but you're wrong, I do know you," Risilan said. "There is no better way to become acquainted with someone than by throwing them into the crucible of battle. From that test of mettle, I know you are honorable and righteous. That you live up to your word."

"That still doesn't explain why," Jason said. "There has to be more."

"It would secure the bonds of allegiance between our two worlds," Risilan said. "Ensuring that we pooled our resources to stave off the coming visitations of the empire to both of our worlds, and those who would serve them."

"Except I don't represent my world," Jason said. "Tying the knot with me would grant you the allegiance of nobody, except the robot army with me."

"Perhaps now," Risilan said. "But eventually, you would return to your planet as our emissary, and secure a treaty of allegiance. I foresee this. But even if not, your present army is good enough for me. You fight with heart. Something that can be said for only a few member species of the empire."

He sighed, gazed out at the lake for a moment, and then returned his attention to her.

"Let's say I agree," Jason told her. "And become king. Your people would accept me?"

She nodded. "They would have to."

"I have a feeling the average Tyrnari isn't all that different from the average human," Jason said. "I'm a robot. Operated by an organic consciousness embedded in an AI core. A consciousness from another planet. I'm not even Tyrnari."

"My people are very open-minded," Risilan said.

"While that may be so, some would revolt," Jason insisted.

"Perhaps," Risilan said. "But the involved parties would be suppressed."

"You're a cruel ruler," Jason said.

"I can be," Risilan agreed. "The weak-willed cannot be queen. They would not last a month, if that."

"What about assassination attempts?" Jason said.

"I will ensure you are safe," Risilan said. "We have surveillance tech here unlike anything your race possesses. Would-be assassins would never reach you."

"Somehow I doubt that." Jason thought a moment longer.

He remembered the arguments Aria and Xin had made for staying, about how humanity would just hunt them down anyway, and how they would be safe, here, living under the auspices of a queen.

But he couldn't do it.

"It's tempting, but I can't," Jason said. "My place is on Earth. And I'm not the monogamous type anymore.

I couldn't give up my other girls to become an alien's mate."

Risilan bit her lower lip, as if she was going to concede even that, and allow him to share, but then she lowered her gaze. He spotted sadness in her eyes before she did so.

"As far as I'm concerned, those girls are my queens already," Jason continued into the silence that followed. "And the little plot of land we call home? That's my kingdom. It's not as big as yours, and doesn't have the space navy, nor anywhere near the troops, but it's mine. So my answer is no."

"I understand." Risilan looked up shyly. "Then at least let me give you your parting gift…"

"Oh?"

She came close, wrapped her arms behind his neck, and kissed him.

"It is a gift you will never forget," Risilan said, her cheeks reddening. She kissed him again, even more passionately.

She was right. The sex that followed was something he would carry with him for the rest of his days, if only for the sheer vigor and enthusiasm on her part.

When he returned to the real world, he found her mech standing before him next to the ruins of the palace. She offered him a small triangular object. There were small hieroglyphics on the surfaces, with pulsing blue veins along the edges.

Jason accepted. "What's this?"

"It will create a rift to my palace, from anywhere in

the galaxy," Risilan said. "Use it to return here if ever you have need."

"Nice." Jason accepted the device, and shoved it into his storage compartment. Then he turned to go.

"What did she want?" Tara asked.

"Tell you later," Jason said.

JASON LED the troops into the forest. After four hours, the sprawling oaks swapped out with the smaller psychedelic pines, and in another four hours they emerged from the forest and reached the rift site. The journey transpired without incident—they didn't encounter any roving bioweapons, or Imperials.

As promised, when the Earth troops stepped out onto the plains, a tear in reality began to form ahead of them. It started out as a purplish gray mist that expanded outward until the interior pinched and distorted the landscape that lay beyond it. The purple fringe continued to expand, until it was one kilometer in length, and eight hundred in height. The rift solidified, and the distortion vanished, replaced by the familiar bleak, rocky plain they'd left behind.

"Well, good old Earth," Jerry said. "Can't say I missed it."

"I did," Jason said.

"Me, too," Lori added.

"Now would be a good time to recall the bombers and jets you parked outside the forest," Jason said.

"Unless you want to give the Modlenth a fully intact set of human aircraft to reverse engineer."

"No thanks," Bokerov said.

"Are the units even intact?" Tara said. "Or did the roving bioweapons get to them?"

"They're intact," Bokerov said.

Jason sent his Explorer drone forward, with instructions to return after performing a quick search of the area. Risilan promised she'd keep the rift open for ten minutes.

The Explorer returned shortly, and Jason reviewed the data. "All right, it looks safe on the other side," Jason said. "No machines, Imperial or human, waiting in ambush. And no mutant bioweapons nearby. Bokerov, where are your craft?"

A moment later the roar of the jets and bombers came overhead, and the craft swooped low to dive through the opening.

"All right, the rest of you, we enter," Jason said.

He led the War Forgers and the clones through. On the other side, the Rex Wolves pranced around happily when they realized where they were.

Home.

Bokerov's contingent followed in organized ranks, with the tanks first, and the Cataphracts bringing up the rear.

Jason glanced at his overhead map on the other side. His positional data updated, courtesy of the repeaters Bokerov had spread throughout the region, setting him at almost the precise spot he had stood on when he departed Earth.

He checked for signs of enemy troops, which would have been detected by the bombers and jets by now, but there were none.

Jason zoomed out on the map, and focused on the mountainous area to the southeast of the country. One of those mountain ranges was directly west of their current location.

He waited until most of Bokerov's tanks had passed through, and then he said: "So, Bokerov, you have a few bases in the mountains... I want you to highlight the one you believe is the most extensive, and secure."

Jason accepted Bokerov's location share request, and zoomed out on the map. The coordinates were roughly a hundred kilometers to the west, nestled amid the mountains there.

Jason shared the location with the other War Forgers. "This will become our new base. Aria, you'll work with your clones to reinforce it, and improve the defenses. We have to prepare for the day when the governments of humanity send a delegation to visit us."

"It won't be a delegation," Xin said softly. "It will be hunter killers."

"Either way, I want to make sure we're ready," Jason said. "I want them to understand that we just want to be left alone."

"We should have stayed on the Tyrnari home-world," Jerry said. "You should have accepted the empress's offer."

"Except that wasn't our homeworld," Jason said. "This is."

Jason had told his other clones of the offer the

empress had made, but he hadn't yet informed the girls. The expected question came a moment later.

"What offer?" Lori asked.

"She wanted me to marry her, and become king," Jason said.

"Gah!" Sophie said. "Thankfully you didn't choose that option. Married to a sickly tentacled alien? What kind of a life is that?"

"He didn't accept, because of us!" Lori said.

"That's right," Jason said. "I refused to give you up."

"Aw," Tara said.

"He can be sweet when he wants to be, can't he?" Aria said.

Jason would have been blushing if he were still human.

"All right then," Jason said. "As soon as all the troops are through, we're heading west, to the mountains. It's time to live out our lives in peace and quiet, instead of fighting through every day."

"At least for the moment," Julian said. "Until the governments of humanity, as you call them, decide to show up."

"We'll deal with that when it comes," Jason said.

Jason watched as the last of Bokerov's Cataphracts entered from the rift.

"What do we do with Bokerov?" Sophie said on a private line that excluded the Russian.

"He stays with us, for now," Jason said. "Lori has already firmed up his Containment Code, in case you're worried he'll turn on us again."

"That's one of my worries," Sophie said. "But I also mean, we can't keep him a slave forever. No matter what he's done, it's not right."

"I would disagree," Aria 5 said. "As far as I'm concerned, what he did to us warrants permanent slavery."

"I have to side with Sophie on this," Jason said. "We can't keep him a slave forever. We'll transfer his mind copies into custom-designed androids at some point, and send him off to Russia. We'll replace any empty tank and Cataphract AI cores with autonomous units."

"To do that, we'll have to gather parts and materials from Bokerov's other bases," Tara said.

"We'll do whatever it takes," Jason said. "But for now, I just want to forget about the future, and enjoy this moment. We've saved Earth, even though humanity might not know it yet, and helped out another alien race in the process, making allies for life. I think we've done pretty well for ourselves, considering we're not even human anymore."

"We certainly have," Xin said.

The rift closed beside them. Jason turned toward the west, facing the location of their new home.

Ahead, the sun was setting.

"Man, I can't tell you how much I really missed sunsets," Tara said, scratching Bruiser under the neck beside her. The Rex Wolf half closed his eyes in delight.

"As did I," Cheyanne said. "And this one is spectacularly beautiful."

"It is indeed," Jason said. The clouds were cast a

pretty purple sandwiched between the reds and yellows of the sky.

He led the War Forgers and his army across the plains, into the setting sun.

Thank you very much for reading!

If you liked this series, consider checking out the AI Reborn trilogy, set sixty years before the events in Battle Harem. Learn about the alien invasion that created the uninhabited zone, and follow the adventures of the brave platoon of Mind Refurbs who sacrificed almost everything to save their human creators.

Get The Next Book

AFTERWORD

Please help spread the word about *Battle Harem 3* by leaving a one or two sentence review. The number of reviews an ebook receives has a big impact on how well it does, so if you liked this story I'd REALLY appreciate it if you left a quick review. Anything will do, even one or two lines.

Thank you!

ABOUT THE AUTHOR

 *USA Today* bestselling author Isaac Hooke holds a degree in engineering physics, though his more unusual inventions remain fictive at this time. He is an avid hiker, cyclist, and photographer who sometimes resides in Edmonton, Alberta.

Get in touch:
isaachooke.com
isaac@isaachooke.com

 facebook.com/isaachookeauthor

twitter.com/isaachooke

ACKNOWLEDGMENTS

I'd also like to thank my knowledgeable beta readers and advanced reviewers who helped smooth out the rough edges of the prerelease manuscript: Nicole P., Lisa G., Gary F., Sandy G., Amy B., Karen J., Jeremy G., Doug B., Jenny O., Bryan O., Lezza, Noel, Anton, Spencer, Norman, Trudi, Corey, Erol, Terje, David, Charles, Walter, Lisa, Ramon, Chris, Scott, Michael, Chris, Bob, Jim, Maureen, Zane, Chuck, Shayne, Anna, Dave, Roger, Nick, Gerry, Charles, Annie, Patrick, Mike, Jeff, Lisa, Jason, Bryant, Janna, Tom, Jerry, Chris, Jim, Brandon, Kathy, Norm, Jonathan, Derek, Shawn, Judi, Eric, Rick, Bryan, Barry, Sherman, Jim, Bob, Ralph, Darren, Michael, Chris, Michael, Julie, Glenn, Rickie, Rhonda, Neil, Claude, Ski, Joe, Paul, Larry, John, Norma, Jeff, David, Brennan, Phyllis, Robert, Darren, Daniel, Montzalee, Robert, Dave, Diane, Peter, Skip, Louise, Dave, Brent, Erin, Paul, Jeremy, Dan,

Garland, Sharon, Dave, Pat, Nathan, Max, Martin, Greg, David, Myles, Nancy, Ed, David, Karen, Becky, Jacob, Ben, Don, Carl, Gene, Bob, Luke, Teri, Robine, Gerald, Lee, Rich, Ken, Daniel, Chris, Al, Andy, Tim, Robert, Fred, David, Mitch, Don, Tony, Dian, Tony, John, Sandy, James, David, Pat, Gary, Jean, Bryan, William, Roy, Dave, Vincent, Tim, Richard, Kevin, George, Andrew, John, Richard, Robin, Sue, Mark, Jerry, Rodger, Rob, Byron, Ty, Mike, Gerry, Steve, Benjamin, Anna, Keith, Jeff, Josh, Herb, Bev, Simon, John, David, Greg, Larry, Timothy, Tony, Ian, Niraj, Maureen, Jim, Len, Bryan, Todd, Maria, Angela, Gerhard, Renee, Pete, Hemantkumar, Tim, Joseph, Will, David, Suzanne, Steve, Derek, Valerie, Laurence, James, Andy, Mark, Tarzy, Christina, Rick, Mike, Paula, Tim, Jim, Gal, Anthony, Ron, Dietrich, Mindy, Ben, Steve, Allen, Paddy & Penny, Troy, Marti, Herb, Jim, David, Alan, Leslie, Chuck, Dan, Perry, Chris, Rich, Rod, Trevor, Rick, Michael, Tim, Mark, Alex, John, William, Doug, Tony, David, Sam, Derek, John, Jay, Tom, Bryant, Larry, Anjanette, Gary, Travis, Jennifer, Henry, Drew, Michelle, Bob, Gregg, Billy, Jack, Lance, Sandra, Libby, Jonathan, Karl, Bruce, Clay, Gary, Sarge, Andrew, Deborah, Steve, and Curtis.

Without you all, this novel would have typos, continuity errors, and excessive lapses in realism. Thank you for helping me make this the best novel possible, and thank you for leaving the early reviews that help new readers find my books.

And of course I'd be remiss if I didn't thank my

mother, father, and brothers, whose wisdom and insights have always guided me through the winding roads of life.

— Isaac Hooke

Made in the USA
San Bernardino, CA
15 February 2019